The Battle for the Bar-Q

Mitch Evans is riding to his brother's small ranch after receiving a telegram saying there was trouble brewing. But Cal Morgan, a ranch hand for the Bar-Q, has been forced by his ruthless foreman, Latham Parry, to ambush Mitch before he can get to his brother's ranch, the Bar-B.

Both men shoot each other – Mitch in the shoulder and Cal in the leg. So begins an unlikely friendship that will endure pain and hardship as well as love.

All in the name of the Bar-Q.

The Battle for the Bar-Q

Will Black

A Black Horse Western

ROBERT HALE

© Will Black 2018
First published in Great Britain 2018

ISBN 978-0-7198-2861-4

The Crowood Press
The Stable Block
Crowood Lane
Ramsbury
Marlborough
Wiltshire SN8 2HR

www.bhwesterns.com

Robert Hale is an imprint
of The Crowood Press

Typeset by
Derek Doyle & Associates, Shaw Heath
Printed and bound in Great Britain by
4Bind Ltd, Stevenage, SG1 2XT

To Sam and Sophie, my Nephew and Niecey.

CHAPTER ONE

The gunshot came out of the blue.

Just a minute before the lone rider had been admiring the spring scenery in all its glory – cottonwoods in bud, yucca in bloom, ferrocactus with their red tops, looking as though they were on fire, and a wide variety of wild flowers. In the distance the mountains of the Sierra Nevada rose majestically to embrace the brilliant blue of the cloudless sky.

The slug caught Mitch Evans in the left shoulder. It was a lucky shot, skimming off the bone before it could do any real damage. Instinctively Mitch threw himself to the right, grabbing his Winchester as he thudded to the ground. The jolt sent a spasm of sharp pain coursing through his body, but he ignored it. He had to.

A second shot smashed into the ground beside him; he didn't flinch and didn't move a muscle. He knew his very survival lay in the next few minutes. Whoever was shooting at him needed to be sure he was dead, or at least unconscious. Straining his ears, he picked up the sound of pebbles falling down the bluff to his left, and then the

7

sound of boots crunching the soil as the bushwhacker made his way to his expected prize.

Mitch heard the lever action of a rifle loading another slug into the breach, and he moved his right hand till he felt the butt of his Colt. Easing back the hammer, he waited. Sweat oozed from every pore in his body, some caused by the sun's heat, but most from the throbbing pain in his left shoulder.

Yet still he didn't move. He hadn't ridden all this way for it to end here.

He felt, rather than saw, a shadow move briefly across his eyes and knew his assailant was towering over him. He knew for certain when he felt a boot nudged his body to see if he was conscious. Then he made his move.

Faster than the eye could see, Mitch drew and fired. The slug caught his assailant in the kneecap, sending the man backwards, screaming. Mitch managed to raise himself on one knee, his gun still trained on the figure writhing in agony and gripping his contorted leg above the knee, trying to staunch the blood.

Still on one knee, Mitch scanned the bluff before him, unsure if there was anyone else up there. He saw no movement or tell-tale glint of sunlight reflecting off metal.

'So, you're alone, mister,' he said through gritted teeth at the prostrate man. The man didn't answer.

'You want the other knee shot off?' Mitch asked, cocking the Colt.

Sweat was pouring down the injured man's face, and from out of nowhere, flies began to land on the slowly spreading pool of blood beneath his leg. He was panting heavily, his teeth gritted together as he fought to control the pain.

'Alone. I'm alone,' he managed to say. Mitch stood up and scanned the territory, looking for his horse. He let out a piercing whistle, and within minutes the sound of pounding hoofs could be heard as his mount returned. Grabbing the reins, Mitch mounted up.

'You ain't leaving me here, are you?'

'You tell me what I need to know and we'll see,' Mitch said.

'What . . . what do you need to know?'

'Who you are? Why d'you try to bushwhack me? And who sent you?'

The man didn't answer straightaway. Beads of sweat from both the heat and the pain ran down his face. The pool of blood around his leg grew ever larger. Mitch knew that unless he staunched the blood with a tourniquet soon, the man would simply bleed to death. The man knew this as well.

'My name's Cal Morgan,' he eventually said.

'That's one question answered. Two to go,' Mitch stated.

'I work for the Bar-Q ranch.'

'Yeah, I know it, twenty miles from here,' Mitch said. 'So Josh Winters sent you.'

'No – not exactly.'

'Not exactly?'

'No.'

'You ain't got much time left, mister,' Mitch said.

'It was . . . it was Latham Parry.'

'An' who's he?' Mitch asked.

9

'He's Winters' foreman,' Morgan replied.

'Go on,' Mitch said flatly.

'Can we sort my leg out, mister? I'm losing a lot of blood here.'

Mitch considered the question for a few moments, then decided the man was desperate enough to keep telling the truth, so he dismounted.

Taking off his bandanna, he tied it tightly round the man's thigh.

'Best I can do,' Mitch said as he stood up. 'Now tell me the rest of the story.'

'That's all I know,' Morgan said through gritted teeth. 'I was given twenty dollars by Parry to shoot you. He gave no reason. And Parry is not the sort of man you refuse.'

'So you'd kill for twenty dollars?' Mitch couldn't hide his disgust.

'Mister, if I'd refused Parry would have killed me for sure.'

'Ain't so sure I ain't gonna kill you now,' Mitch replied.

The look on Morgan's face was one of resignation. 'If I don't get to a doc soon, you won't have to,' he said through a wave of pain.

'Where's your horse?' Mitch asked.

'Behind the bluff,' Morgan pointed. Without a word Mitch mounted up and rode his horse up the small slope, disappearing from view.

Morgan watched him leave, hoping it was to get his animal. At least mounted, if he could manage it, he'd have a chance to ride into town and get some doctoring.

Five minutes passed and Morgan was getting edgy.

Maybe the fella has ridden off, he thought. Sweat was pouring from him now, and the pain was almost unbearable. He was at the point of giving up all hope when Mitch returned, leading Morgan's horse. Dismounting and ground hitching both animals, Mitch removed his Stetson, wiped the sweatband and put it back on.

'I can't mount up on my own,' Morgan moaned.

'I still want to know why you tried to bushwhack me,' Mitch said, resting his right hand on the butt of his pistol.

'I tole you already.'

'You told me who sent you, but not why,' Mitch said between gritted teeth.

'I don't know why. I was just told to take you out.'

'That don't make no sense,' Mitch said. 'I've never been here before.'

Despite the pain, Cal asked: 'Where are you headed?'

'Got a telegram from my brother, seems like he's got himself a whole mess o' trouble brewin' and needed some help.'

'Would that be Brad Evans?' Cal asked.

'You know him?'

'Sure – well, I know of him, he owns a spread just south of here, the Bar-B,' Cal replied.

'This got anything to do with your boss?'

'Honest, mister, I ain't sure. Ol' Josh is getting on in years, but a better boss you'd go a long way to find. It's Latham who's running the show, an' he ain't satisfied with just bein' a foreman, I can tell you that.'

'So it's land-grabbin', is it?' Mitch said almost to himself.

'Mister, I need to get to a doc, pronto.'

'OK. I'll help you mount up,' Mitch dismounted and stood behind the stricken man.

'When I lift you, stand on your good leg.'

'I won't be able to lift my right leg,' Cal said.

'Don't worry, I'll lift it for you.'

It took Mitch some effort to lift the man aboard his pony, as the wound in his shoulder hampered his movement, but eventually he got him in the saddle.

'How far's the nearest town?' Mitch asked, mounting up himself.

'Calvary – it's about ten or twelve miles south-east of here.'

'OK. You lead the way, an' no funny stuff, you got that?'

'Mister, if'n I survive this, you won't see hair nor hide of me agen. I can't go back to the Bar-Q, Parry will kill me for sure.'

Doc Mayweather was a larger-than-life character – and large in every sense of the word. He stood six feet five inches in his stockinged feet, and had a stomach you could fit a saddle on. A large, purple-coloured nose was the main feature of his face, a testament to his love of whiskey, and deep brown eyes, above which grew a forest of hairy eyebrows, which in turn led to a full head of dark brown hair. He stared over half-spectacles at the two men who entered his surgery unannounced.

'He's got a leg shot,' Mitch said.

'He's hit in the shoulder,' Cal added.

'What in hell you boys been up to?' Mayweather bellowed. His voice was as big as his frame.

'Well, I shot his kneecap,' Mitch muttered.

'An' I nicked his shoulder,' Cal said, leaning heavily on Mitch.

'Playin' cowboys and Indians?' Mayweather laughed.

'I'm bleedin' to death here, Doc,' Cal said through clenched teeth.

'OK, OK. Let's get him on the table,' Mayweather grabbed Cal under the arm, and between them they laid him down. Grabbing a large pair of scissors that looked more like shears, Mayweather began cutting Cal's denims straight up the middle.

'Dammit, Doc, them's the only pants I got!' Cal groaned.

'If'n I don't stop this bleedin' pretty damn quick you won't need two pants legs, mister!' Mayweather continued cutting.

Mitch sat in the corner of the surgery and rolled himself a cigarette; he was just about to strike a Lucifer when Mayweather turned on him.

'You wanna kill yourself, go outside. I don't allow smoking in here!'

'Smoking's good for you, Doc, you know that,' Mitch countered.

'Tell that to your lungs, boy,' Mayweather replied. 'No smoking in here.'

Reluctantly Mitch got to his feet and shuffled outside. Although late in the day, he guessed it was around four in the afternoon; the sun still shone brightly in the west. There were no clouds, just a heat haze, and the gold orb of the sun was impossible to look at unless you wanted to go blind.

Mitch lowered his gaze and looked about the small town. One street, and that was it. What breeze there was raised dust from the parched earth. Just another one-horse town. He guessed that if it wasn't for the surrounding ranches, Calvary wouldn't even exist.

There was a small saloon, a livery, a mercantile, which probably did the most business in town, and a gun shop with a sign hanging off rope, swaying in the breeze, that declared 'New and used and we repair 'em too'.

Apart from a small café, the rest of the street was filled with wooden shacks, around ten or twelve, all exactly the same.

He saw no sign of a sheriff's office or jail. Must have no need, he thought.

Mitch finished his smoke and tossed the glowing butt into the street. Not a soul was visible, and if he didn't know better, he would have thought it was a ghost town.

The pain in his shoulder had subsided to a dull ache. It was stiff, but bearable. Turning, Mitch walked back into the doc's surgery.

'How's he doin', Doc?' Mitch asked.

'He'll live. I stopped the bleeding. He was lucky, the bullet missed the patella . . .' – he saw the look on the two men's faces – '. . . the kneecap, but sure made a mess of some ligaments. Can't repair them.'

'Will I be able to walk, Doc?' Cal asked.

'You'll be able to walk, but that leg ain't gonna bend no more. Be as stiff as a broom-pole.'

'Well, that's better than losing the leg,' Mitch piped up.

'You'll need to keep off that leg for at least a month.

14

I'll lend you a crutch. Come back in a week and I'll change the dressings. That'll be twenty dollars,' Mayweather said as he turned and washed the blood off his hands.

'Heck, Doc, I ain't got no more'n ten dollars to my name,' Cal said, shamefaced.

'I'll take care of it,' Mitch said. 'Check my shoulder over, Doc, and I'll pay.'

'Mighty generous of you,' Cal looked relieved.

'Oh, you'll work for it. You got no place to go, so we'll head out to the Bar-B as soon as I'm fixed up,' Mitch said with a wry grin.

The wound in Mitch's left shoulder, although deep, was clean, and the damage more painful than dangerous. The doc patched it up and put Mitch's arm in a sling.

'It'll be sore for a while and a tad stiff, but you should be OK within a couple of weeks. Try not to use the arm overly,' Mayweather said. 'That's twenty-five dollars all in, and I'll throw in a bottle of laudnum, but use it sparingly, OK?'

'Thanks, Doc,' both men said almost together.

'Could you give me a hand getting Cal into the saddle, Doc?'

'Sure thing.'

'There a hotel or boarding-house in town, Doc?' Mitch asked,

'Sure. Ellie-Rae sometimes lets a room out. It's over the café. She cooks a mighty fine steak pie, too. Tell her I sent you over.'

Once saddled, the two men bade the doc farewell and set off to the café.

'Fine pair we are,' Cal said, 'me with one leg and you with one arm.'

'Well, at least we ain't dead,' Mitch replied.

'Yet,' Cal added.

CHAPTER TWO

Josh Winters was well aware he was losing control of both his foreman and his ranch. Wheelchair-bound after a riding accident, he was totally reliant on his housekeeper, Maria Gonzalez, for his every need. Latham Parry, the foreman, had collected a set of men more used to gunplay than herding cattle or busting broncos. He had big plans for the Bar-Q, and he was a ruthless killer and manipulator who would let nothing get in his way. His plan was simple and as old as the hills: get rid of the smaller ranches that surrounded the Bar-Q, by fair means or foul – and the word 'fair' was not in his vocabulary.

The Bar-Q was some 30,000 acres, situated between Lubbock to the north and Midland to the south, most of it prime grassland fed by the Colorado river. Josh Winters had founded the ranch some thirty years ago, fighting off Indians and claim jumpers as well as the elements. Initially to breed and raise horses for the army as well as the surrounding towns, he soon saw the profit to be made from cattle. Once established, and with a small ranch house built, he sent for his childhood sweetheart,

Anne-Marie, from Galveston on the banks of the Gulf of Mexico, to join him and become his wife. But the stage she was on was raided by Indians between Houston and Waco, and it was six months before Josh learned what had happened.

He never married, and had no heir to his ranch and vast fortune. Most of his original and faithful crew were either dead, or in a worse state than he was. With his heart broken, he devoted all his energy into building up a herd. The ranch house was expanded and the herd grew. Soon his beef was in high demand, and the regular drives to Abilene and on to Dallas earned him more money than he could ever spend.

Maria Gonzalez had crossed the Rio Grande at Del Rio when she was eighteen years old, to escape the poverty they lived in, and also the threat her parents had made that she would be sold and married to the highest bidder. The journey was arduous as well as dangerous, but her desire to rule her own life, and her strength of purpose, saw her through. She slowly made her way to Odessa, getting any job she could to keep body and soul together. Eventually she reached Lubbock – and that's where Josh Winters found her.

Josh had driven his buckboard into Lubbock at around three in the afternoon. His plan was to pick up supplies, grab something to eat, and get back to the ranch before nightfall. His supplies were ready and waiting for him, and the storekeeper and his lad helped him load the buckboard.

'Thanks, Jim,' Josh said to the storekeeper and tossed a dollar to the lad who helped out after school.

'Gee, thanks mister,' the boy said, his eyes wide as he saw the gleaming coin in his hand.

'What's that new eatery like, Jim?' Josh asked.

'Mighty fine,' Jim replied. 'Best stew and dumplings I ever did eat, and the apple pie just melts in your mouth.'

'Sounds good to me,' Josh said. 'OK if I leave the buckboard here?'

'Sure,' Jim said, 'we'll keep an eye on it.'

'Thanks.'

Josh made his way down Main Street, slapping the trail dust off his clothes as he went. It was then he heard a muffled scream. He stood stock still, trying to fathom where the sound had come from. He took his Stetson off and cocked his head to one side, trying to cut out the noises on the street.

The muffled scream came again, and Josh ducked down a side alley. The shadows were deep and black, but he could just make out the outlines of three figures, two men and a woman. Josh immediately drew his Colt, and shouted: 'What in hell's goin' on here?'

The struggling stopped briefly as a gruff and obviously drunk voice bellowed: 'Mind yer business, mister.'

'I'm making it my business,' Josh yelled. 'Let that woman go. *Now!*'

In the deep gloom of the alley Josh saw one man break free from the woman, and as his eyes had become used to the darkness, he saw him reach for his gun. Josh didn't hesitate: he aimed low and hit the man in the leg before he could pull the trigger.

Immediately, the other man drew, but Josh held his fire as he still had hold of the woman and his pistol was

19

pressed to her head.

'Don't do anything stupid, fella,' Josh cautioned. 'Take your pal and walk away.'

'Oh, I'm walking away all right, and this li'l filly is walking with me. You just go about your business, cowboy, an' no one will get hurt.'

'That ain't gonna happen, fella,' Josh said, his Colt held steady in his right hand.

'Jed,' the injured man croaked, 'let's just get out of here. I'm hurtin' real bad here.'

'Shut your mouth, I ain't backin' down to no green-horn!' But as the man said this, his attention was momentarily taken away from Josh, and it was all that Josh needed to make his play.

Maria seemed to sense that, one way or another, the situation was about to end, and instinctively she stamped on her captor's foot as hard as she could. The man's gun arm dropped slightly, and without a second's hesitation, Josh fired. The .45 slug caught the man called Jed in the upper arm, shattering the humerus from the collarbone, and the man screamed; he stood in shock for a few seconds as his right arm fell useless to his side.

Maria slumped to the ground, and for an instant, Josh thought his shot had hit her. Rushing over, he knelt by her side, and was relieved to see a small smile on her lips and her large brown eyes peering up at him.

'Thank you, *señor*, you saved my life!'

That was forty years ago, and Maria had devoted her life to Josh Winters ever since. Sitting in his wheelchair, Josh found himself dwelling more on the past than the present; the future didn't even enter his head.

*

Now that the trail drive had started, two and a half thousand head of prime beef on the hoof, the only hands left on the ranch were Parry's hand-picked men – or rather, men whom Clancy had selected for the next operation that Parry had in mind.

Latham Parry was outlining his plan for the raid on the Bar-B that night. 'Plan' was perhaps too grand a word for it. Brad Evans was one of the many thorns Parry had in his side. The Bar-B was fine grazing land, and Parry saw it as the first step to building his empire. Old man Winters was too old and too frail to stop him, and Parry knew his days were numbered. With no family to inherit the Bar-Q, Parry would simply take it over.

But Parry was not a patient man, and had already taken steps to ensure that Winters' time would be up soon. Real soon.

CHAPTER THREE

Mitch reined in outside the café and tied his horse to the hitch rail.

'Hang on here, I'll go an' get us a room,' he said to Cal.

Cal nodded. Although the laudanum was beginning to work, he was still in a lot of pain. Mitch opened the door to the café and immediately the smell of food filled his nostrils. It was then he realized he hadn't eaten for at least twelve hours and his belly was now reminding him of that fact.

The café was small – a quick glance and Mitch counted six tables, five of which were occupied. A red-headed woman approached him wearing an apron, her hair piled high on her head; she looked him over with eyes as green as grass. Hurriedly, Mitch took off his Stetson and held it in both hands in front of him.

'Only got pie and greens left, mister,' she said, her ruby-red lips revealing teeth as white as snow. Like a fool, Mitch stood there with his mouth open.

Ellie-Rae put her hands on her hips. 'You dumb, mister?'

'No. No I ain't. Sorry. I . . . well . . . I . . . pie and greens would be good. Great, I mean, yes. An' a room. Doc sent us over.'

'Us?' Ellie-Rae cocked an eyebrow, a faint trace of amusement on her face at Mitch's embarrassment.

'Sorry, ma'am, my, er, partner is outside. Got himself a bullet in the leg. I just wanted to make sure there was a room here for us before I help him down.'

'You say Doc Mayweather sent you over?' she asked.

'Yes ma'am. He fixed up Cal's leg an' my shoulder.'

'How long you staying?'

'Just the one night, ma'am, if'n that's OK,' Mitch's stomach was still rumbling and he wasn't sure if it was all due to hunger, or being in the presence of a beautiful woman.

'Guess I can accommodate you, Mr . . .?'

'Evans, ma'am. Mitch Evans.'

'You want feedin' too?'

'Oh, yes, ma'am. Ain't eaten in a while.'

'OK, get your partner, I'll rustle up some grub.'

'Thank you kindly, ma'am.'

'An' quit calling me "ma'am". Name's Ellie-Rae O'Hara.'

'Miss O'Hara,' Mitch said as he put his Stetson on the vacant table and went outside to get Cal. Getting Cal off the horse was much easier than getting him on it. Using his crutch, Cal limped into the café and sat down heavily, his right leg stretched out rigid in front of him.

Ellie-Rae returned with two plates piled high with pie

23

and greens, and a plate of fresh sourdough bread.

'Coffee'll be along in a minute,' she said. As she turned to go back into the kitchen she asked, 'So who shot you?'

Mitch jerked a thumb at Cal. 'He did.'

'And you?' Ellie-Rae asked Cal.

'He did.'

'That's just plain loco,' Ellie-Rae said, and vanished into the kitchen.

Cal Morgan's appearance in Calvary hadn't gone unnoticed. One of Parry's stooges, an old-timer called Will – no one knew his last name – watched as Cal and a stranger walked their horses to the doc's place.

Will spent most of his time swamping out the grandly named Palace saloon, cleaning out the spittoons and collecting – and draining – glasses left unattended on the bartop or tables. He also had the amazing knack of converting any nickels, dimes and the occasional dollar into rotgut. But although he might be the town drunk and a laughing stock, he was no fool: he recognized Cal straightaway, and knew he was one of Parry's men. He could also see the blood on the man's leg.

Will licked his lips. Dollar signs flashed into his eyes, and he was consumed with a raging thirst. Latham Parry might slip him a dollar or two for this information, and already Will could see the bottle of rotgut and a shot glass in front of him.

Doc Mayweather was seated on his rocker drinking a glass of lemonade as Will ambled across the street in his direction.

'Evenin', Doc,' Will said affably. 'Been busy, I see.'

'I got no chores for you, Will,' Doc said.

'I ain't after work, Doc. Jus' shootin' the breeze. What's ol' Cal bin up to?'

'Didn't know you knew him,' the doc said.

'Sure, sure I do. One o' Josh's men, ain't he? Don't know the other fella though. He new in these parts?'

'You seem mighty interested in them, Will. Now why would that be?'

'Aw, you know me, Doc, jus' makin' conversation, is all.'

'Well, to put you out of your misery, the other fella is Brad Evans's brother,' the doc added, and took a sip of lemonade.

'That so?' Will mused. 'That so. Well, Doc, better get back to my chores. The devil drives an' all that. Be seein' ya.'

Will ambled round to the rear of the saloon as fast as his bony old legs could carry him, to where the buckboard and pony were kept. The saloon owner, Brett Larson, a not very successful ex-gambler who had had one lucky break when he won the Palace and then quit, had given Will *carte blanche* with the buckboard in lieu of payment, as he used Will to make deliveries and collect supplies.

Will hitched up the pony and headed out to the Bar-Q.

Having finished their meal and relaxing with the last of the coffee, Ellie-Rae asked if they wanted anything else.

'Ma'am – sorry, Miss O'Hara – that sure was a mighty

fine meal.' Mitch rubbed his now full stomach.

'Thank you, that'll be six dollars. Including the meal, bed and breakfast.'

'And worth every penny,' Cal added.

Mitch paid the bill, and Ellie-Rae showed them to their room.

'Thank you, ma' . . . Miss O'Hara – a good night to you,' Mitch said, sounding far more formal than he intended.

The room was small, but looked comfortable. There were two single cots, one on each side of a small table carrying an oil lamp. Against the opposite wall was a small dresser with a bowl and pitcher, and two towels, neatly folded, with a bar of soap on top. Mitch unbuckled his gunbelt and hung it on the bed post, placed his Stetson on top of it, then flopped down on to the bed.

Cal lowered himself down and sat on his bed, resting the crutch against the wall; he, too, unbuckled his gunbelt and slowly lay back.

'Could you just lift my leg on to the bed, Mitch?'

'Sure thing,' Mitch replied.

Once he'd settled Cal, Mitch lay on his own bed and, without lighting the oil lamp, both men fell into an untroubled sleep.

It would turn out to be the last one they had for a while.

It was close on midnight when Latham Parry got his small gang together. The men had coated their hands and faces with axle grease, and each wore a headband with a prominent feather and deerskin clothing. In the dark they would easily be thought of as Indians. To complete the deception, each man had a quiver and a bow slung around his shoulders. It was hoped there would be no gunplay that night.

Silently the seven horsemen, led by Parry, left the Bar-Q and headed for the Bar-B. Because the country was so vast it would take over an hour to reach their target, but they were in no hurry. There was very little light from the moon, and that was ideal for their purpose.

The ride over the grasslands was easy: all they had to do was follow the river, and that would lead them straight to the Bar-B. When they got to around two hundred yards from the ranch house, Parry held up an arm, and, dismounting, the men spread out and walked towards the dark and silent house. Two of them had an oil-soaked cloth wrapped around their arrows. The plan was simple: to burn out Brad Evans and his family.

Loading their bows, the two men sent their now flaming arrows towards the ranch house and watched as sparks flew as the arrows found their target. Within minutes, the dry wooden roof was ablaze, lighting up the dark sky with a flickering orange glow.

Their next target was the front door: two more blazing arrows thudded into it and that, too, burst into flame.

Now there was no escape. Anyone in the house was doomed.

Maria Gonzalez was beside Josh Winters' bed within seconds of hearing him coughing. She'd heard the horsemen ride out and had peered through the drapes in her room and saw what looked like a bunch of Indians.

Then the coughing had started. Maria knew that Josh had very little time left, but the old man never complained and was always ready with a smile whenever she entered the room. She poured him a glass of water, and lifting his head, put the glass to his lips. The water soon soothed his throat and he smiled at Maria.

'I want you to know,' he said with a feeble, croaky voice, 'that I've left everything to you in my will. It's lodged with the lawyer, Amos Kline. He's a good man and an old friend. There's a copy of the will in my safe. You know the combination, so just let Amos know. He's in Lubbock, he'll help you with everything.'

He broke off with a coughing fit, but resumed.

'You must get rid of Parry and his cronies. I've given him too much leeway and I know he's up to no good. So look out for yourself.' He took her hand and gently squeezed it.

Maria, choking back tears she would never let him see, said nothing. There was nothing she could say to the old man she had loved for so long.

Josh closed his eyes and within seconds had fallen back to sleep.

Maria allowed a single tear to run down her face and silently left the room.

It took ten minutes for the ranch-house roof to fall inwards. A giant ball of flame billowed into the night sky and wood sparks flew through the air, landing all around the destroyed house. Soon, small flames sparked in the grassy areas, and Latham Parry smiled.

As the roof caved in, the door to the ranch house flew

open. At first Parry thought the wind created by the collapsing roof had blown it open, but then he saw a sight he knew he'd never forget. A figure stood in the doorway, completely engulfed in flames.

As Parry and his men looked on in horror, the figure began to walk towards them, the steps faltering until the ball of flame sank to its knees and eventually fell face down on the ground.

Parry was the first to break the silence.

'Guess we'll have no trouble from Evans now,' he said, with a smirk on his face. He took out a cigar, struck a Lucifer and inhaled deeply.

CHAPTER FOUR

Mitch woke up as the first rays of the sun broke over the eastern horizon. He couldn't remember the last time he'd slept in a bed, and boy, had he slept well.

He stood and stretched before peering through the drapes at the deserted street below. He splashed water on his face, dried himself off, and immediately put on his gun belt. Behind him, Cal woke up. He coughed a few times, then reached for his makings. Pushing himself up on the bed, he yawned as he rolled himself a cigarette, lit it, inhaled, coughed once more, then said, 'Morning.'

'Mornin', sun's up,' Mitch said, and opened the drapes.

A shaft of sunlight headed straight for Cal's face and he immediately raised a hand to shield his eyes.

'Goddamn! Ain't I in enough pain?' he bellowed, and a cloud of smoke left his mouth as he spoke. Mitch pulled one of the drapes across to cut the light out. He bent down and pulled out a piss-pot from beneath the bed and relieved himself.

'You need this?' he asked Cal.

'Well, if I didn't, I sure do now,' came the grumbled reply. He swung his good leg off the bed, and then lifted the stiff one.

'Need a hand?' Mitch asked.

'I'd rather piss my pants!'

'Suit yourself. I'll check on breakfast,' Mitch said as he left the room, leaving Cal to his own devices.

Halfway down the stairs, the unmistakable smell of frying bacon alerted his taste buds.

'Morning, Miss O'Hara,' he said.

'Call me Ellie,' she said without turning round. 'Coffee's on the stove, help yourself. Bacon, eggs and homemade bread OK?'

'Couldn't want for more,' Mitch said as he poured a cup of coffee.

'Your partner awake?' Ellie asked.

'Yeah, he's . . . er . . . getting ready.' Mitch said.

'He'll need a hand,' she replied.

'No, he'll manage. We'll hear him hopping down soon.'

No sooner had Mitch spoken those words than they heard the thump, thump, thump of Cal coming down. Then a muffled curse as the kitchen door swung open.

'Ya might have helped me,' Cal grumbled.

'You said you'd rather . . .'

'I know what I said, but that was . . .' Cal halted as he caught sight of Ellie-Rae. 'Sorry, mornin', ma'am.'

'Sit yourself down, breakfast is ready,' she replied. 'I'll pour you a coffee.'

'Thank you kindly, ma'am,' Cal said as he plonked himself down at the table.

Mitch smiled to himself as he noticed she didn't ask Cal to call her Ellie.

Ellie placed two plates on the table. 'Help yourselves to coffee,' she said.

'Ain't you joinin' us, ma'am?' Cal asked.

'I got chores to do, mister. This place don't run itself.'

'We'll be outa your hair soon,' Mitch said.

'Where're you heading?' Ellie asked.

'Over to the Bar-B. My brother owns it,' Mitch replied.

'Brad Evans?' Ellie said.

'You know him?' Mitch sounded surprised.

'Sure, everyone knows Brad and his family. He stops by for coffee when he picks up his supplies,' Ellie said. 'Give him my best,' she said and left the kitchen.

The two men finished their breakfast, eating as if they hadn't eaten in days. Mitch stood and poured a second cup of coffee for them both, placing the pot back on the stove. He sat, brought out his makings and rolled a cigarette.

Inhaling deeply, he looked round the kitchen, noting how clean and tidy the place was. As he smoked his thoughts drifted to Ellie-Rae.

He wondered how she'd look with her long hair down instead of piled up in a bun. She sure was pretty. He'd never seen eyes as green as hers, and a figure as cute as – well, it sure was cute.

He pulled himself together, stubbed out the cigarette and got to his feet.

'I'll get the gear and horses together, it's time we headed out.'

Cal merely nodded; his leg was giving him some pain

so he took a swig of the laudnum.

'Don't take too much of that stuff,' Mitch advised.

'I ain't. Pain's a mite sore this morning, is all,' Cal replied.

Fifteen minutes later, Mitch returned. Ellie-Rae was washing dishes and Cal was where he had left him.

'We're ready to leave now, Ellie,' Mitch said, removing his Stetson. 'Thank you kindly for the room an' all.'

'You're welcome, Mitch,' she replied, turning to face him.

Mitch's heart raced as he stared into her eyes. Was there a spark there?

'Give my best to your brother,' she said.

'I will.'

'And call back any time you're passing.'

Mitch's face beamed as he replied, 'I sure will, I sure will.'

Fumbling, he helped Cal to his feet and led him outside to the waiting horses. It took a great deal of effort to get him mounted, but once in the saddle, Mitch wiped the sweat from his face and went back inside to get his hat.

Ellie Rae was drying her hands as she looked up. Again. Mitch's heart beat faster and he knew his face was beginning to redden.

Say something, his brain told him, anything!

'Thank you again, Ellie. I might be back in a few days, if'n that's all right.'

'Sure. I'll be here,' she smiled at his embarrassment, noting his boyish charm. She looked deeply into his dark brown eyes and Mitch thought his legs would give way.

'Safe journey, cowboy,' Ellie said.

Mitch put his Stetson on and smiled. He couldn't think of a damn thing to say! He smiled, turned awkwardly, and went out to his horse as if in a dream. He mounted up and the two men rode off.

Unseen by them, Ellie stood in the doorway and watched them go.

Latham Parry and his men watched as the ranch house burned to the ground, leaving only the stone chimney stack standing, surrounded by blackened timber. Thick smoke bellowed skywards, blotting out the stars, and here and there, flames licked hungrily at whatever would still burn.

Casually, Parry walked over to the still smouldering, charred remains of Brad Evans. Lifting a boot, he kicked the body over on to its back. A grinning, eyeless skull looked up at him, the mouth wide open in a silent scream. Silently Parry flicked his spent butt at the body and pushed his hat back on his head, and an evil grin split his features.

Job done, he thought.

He turned and ambled back to his horse. Mounting up, he called out, 'OK, boys, let's hit the trail.'

He wheeled his horse's head round and set off back to the Bar-Q. The men rode in silence – the full horror of what they had just done was beginning to sink in, and they didn't share Parry's enthusiasm for such a foul deed. They were gunnies, not bushwhackers. They had killed before, some many times, but always in a fair fight, man to man.

This was different. There was nothing fair about burning a man and his family to death, and it was starting to weigh heavily on their minds. But such was the power that Parry had over them – not that any of them would admit it – that they feared him. Each man knew that Parry would kill any or all of them at the drop of a hat just for the hell of it. It was purely the money they were paid that kept them at the Bar-Q.

The eerie blue light of the moon gently gave way to a dull rosy red as the sun began to rise in the east as the men entered the Bar-Q compound.

Maria woke instantly at the sound of so many hoofs. She parted the drapes of her bedroom window and watched as six Indians dismounted.

Panic engulfed her briefly, until she recognized Parry. She watched them dismount, take off their headbands and feathers and then lead their mounts into the barn.

Parry stripped off his buckskins, revealing his usual garb: black shirt and pants. Maria had a bad feeling about this – but who to turn to?

CHAPTER FIVE

Will Garrett, the town's seemingly compulsory drunk, spent the night in the buckboard. Anxious as he was to get to the Bar-Q – he had visions of a handsome reward for his information – the lure of the bottle of rotgut whiskey was stronger, and he drank himself into oblivion. Even seated on the buckboard he lost his balance, dropped the reins and fell to one side. He was out cold. Fortunately for him, the nag that was pulling the buckboard found a clump of grass and was content to stop and eat.

The early morning rays of the sun slapped into Will's face, jerking him awake. His head throbbed, his eyes were bleary, and he wondered where the hell he was. Time for a wake-up drink, he thought.

Opening the second of the two bottles he had 'borrowed' from the saloon, he took a mouthful. The fiery liquid hit the back of his throat like swallowing a bucketful of coarse sand. It burned its way down to his empty stomach and Will shuddered as the effects hit his brain at the same moment.

Shaking his head and rubbing his eyes, Will looked around him for the first time, and slowly, remembered why he was here.

He had news for Latham Parry.

But what the hell was it?

He vaguely remembered brushing the boardwalk outside the saloon, the broom more of a crutch than anything else. Two men! He remembered two men. Then suddenly it all came back to him, and he grabbed the reins: 'Giddup!' he yelled, and slowly, the buckboard inched forwards.

Mitch and Cal walked their horses along the trail that led to both the Bar-B and the Bar-Q, before it split. The left trail led to Mitch's brother's ranch. They rode deliberately slowly as Cal could only manage one foot in the stirrup – his other leg hung stiffly down the horse's side. It seemed that every small jolt hit his bad knee against the hard leather of the Western saddle.

'I gotta hold up a while, Mitch,' Cal said. 'My leg sure is sore.'

'How long afore we reach the Bar-B?' Mitch asked.

'No more'n a couple of hours, I figure. Trail splits about two or three three miles ahead.'

'OK, let's see what I can do about your leg,' Mitch said as he dismounted.

'Keeps hitting the side of the saddle,' Cal explained.

Mitch thought for a while, then came up with a possible solution.

'Well, side saddle is out of the question on a rigid saddle, so although it might be a tad uncomfortable, let's try putting your bedroll under your leg – that'll clear it of the saddle.'

'Uncomfortable beats pain, I reckon,' Cal replied.

It took only a few minutes to secure the bedroll to Cal's leg, moving it free from the saddle.

'Hell, feels like I'm doin' the splits!' Cal moaned.

'Well, it won't bang against this hard leather, so stop your complaining. Let's ride!'

Maria was beside herself with worry. She knew something bad had happened and there was no one she could tell. The only ranch hands nearby were Parry's men; the rest were out on the range preparing the herd for the drive.

Josh was in no condition to be told anything, and even if he wasn't so ill, Maria wouldn't burden him with anything that might cause him further stress. Neither could she ride into town and inform the sheriff: that would entail leaving Josh alone – and vulnerable. She wouldn't put anything past Latham Parry.

She would just have to bide her time and seize any opportunity to get help.

The buckboard carrying Will Garrett pulled up outside the bunkhouse, and Will fell, rather than got down from the driver's seat. A plume of dust rose in the still air as Will's body slumped to the ground. His senses were so numbed by the rotgut whiskey that he felt nothing. All he knew was that the fall had taken the wind out of him, and he couldn't breathe properly for a few minutes. He did feel the boot that caught him on the thigh, though.

'What the hell you doin' here, ol' man?'

Will managed to get himself on his hands and knees, panting, trying to get his breath back. 'Got . . . a . . . message,' he managed to say.

'Spit it out, then,' the man said. 'Ain't got all day.'

'Ain't fer you!' Will spat, 'it's fer Mr Parry.'

'Spit it out ol' man, 'less you don't want to lose your kneecaps!'

'What the hell's this ruckus, Clancy?' Latham Parry shouted as he stormed out of the bunkhouse.

'Mr Parry . . .' Will began.

'What you want, Will?' Parry didn't like being woken up. 'It had better be important.'

'Sure makes a man thirsty, gettin' out here,' Will said.

'You stink o' booze, old man. Get him some water, Clancy – a lot of water,' Parry said.

Clancy grinned as he got the inference. 'Sure thing, boss.'

Five minutes later, Clancy returned with a bucket. 'Here ya go, ol' man, plenty here to drink.'

So saying he emptied the contents of the bucket over Will.

Will coughed and spluttered, 'Weren't no need fer that!'

'Say what you gotta say and git the hell out of here,' Parry said, standing menacingly over Will.

Scrambling to his feet, Will said, 'I figured you might be interested in what I see'd in town.'

'Old man, if'n you don't spit it out soon I'm gonna run out of patience!'

'Figured it must be worth the price of a bottle or two,' Will added.

Parry drew his Colt and cocked the hammer. 'I'll be the judge of that!'

Will hesitated for a mere second before saying: 'I saw Cal ride into town with a stranger, they was both wounded. I asked the doc who the stranger was.'

'And?' Parry said between gritted teeth.

'It was Brad Evans's brother.'

Almost imperceptibly, Parry's eyes narrowed and hardened, but Will saw the expression change and smiled inwardly.

Wordlessly, Parry uncocked the Colt and holstered it. He then reached into his vest pocket and withdrew two dollar coins, which he threw to the ground in front of Will.

'Now get your ass outa here,' Parry said and went back inside the bunkhouse.

Clancy snorted and followed his boss. Will grabbed the coins and clambered back on to the buckboard. All that was on his mind was the two bottles of rotgut the coins would buy.

Maria had watched the whole episode unfold, and although she couldn't hear what was being said, it was obvious at the outcome that the old man had passed on a message to Latham Parry that was of interest.

She quickly scribbled a note and rushed across the compound to catch Will before he left.

'Wait!' she called out, and Will reined in. 'Please give this note to Doctor Mayweather, it's urgent.'

Will put the note in his vest pocket; he didn't open it as he couldn't read. Maria smiled, and handed him a dollar coin. Will's face broke into a wide grin: three bottles, he thought, as he tipped his hat and set off back to Calvary.

Latham Parry stood in the doorway of the bunkhouse smoking, trying to calm his anger at what he thought of as a betrayal by Cal Morgan. Damn him to hell! He inhaled deeply, and then his attention was caught by the sight of Josh's housekeeper running across the courtyard. He watched as she slipped something into Will's hand.

'Now what the hell?' Parry said out loud. 'Clancy! I got a job for you.'

Mitch and Cal were making steady progress along the trail. By now, the sun was at its height and the heat intense.

'Sure could do with a break,' Cal said. The effort of staying in the saddle was exhausting.

'OK. There's a clump of cottonwoods just off the trail, they'll give us some shade. I got bread an' beans and a whole bunch of coffee,' Mitch said as he pointed towards the trees, which were about a hundred yards off the trail.

'Sounds good to me,' Cal said, and the relief in his voice was evident. The two men walked their horses across the rough, knee-high grass and reined in under the cottonwoods. A gentle breeze rustled the grassland, and the shade afforded the men some relief. Mitch dismounted and helped Cal out of the saddle and up against one of the trees.

Cal sank gratefully to the ground and Mitch began gathering wood to build a fire. Within ten minutes he had the fire going, and with the coffee on to boil, they ate the beans cold, soaking them up with the bread. When they finished eating, Mitch poured the coffee and the two men rolled a quirly and relaxed.

Pretty soon, both men fell into a light slumber.

'You called me, boss?' Clancy said, pulling on his gun belt.

'Yeah, that housekeeper woman just handed a note to ol' Will. I don't trust her none. Would be mighty handy to see what the note said.' Parry didn't have to say more.

'On my way, boss.'

Clancy saddled up and rode out of the Bar-Q. Parry watched him leave with a grin on his face.

Maria watched him go too, filled with a sense of foreboding.

Clancy was in no hurry. He wanted to catch up with Will on the open range, not on Bar-Q land, so for a while he kept his horse to a walk. He even had time to roll a cigarette and enjoy the ride. In the distance he could see the dust cloud sent up by the buckboard. In less than a mile, Will would be off Bar-Q land. Clancy finished his cigarette and tossed it away, setting his horse to a canter. It didn't take long for him to pull up alongside the buckboard.

Will had heard nothing of his approach: his mind was on rotgut, his eyes focused on the trail ahead, and his hearing wasn't what it used to be. So when Clancy showed up he nearly had palpitations.

'What the hell you sneakin' up on me fer?' Will blustered. 'Damn near scart me half to death!'

'Hold your horses, old timer. You got somethin' Mr

42

Parry wants,' Clancy said, and Will noticed his right arm hanging down by his holster.

'Dang! He don't want his money back, do he?' Will was alarmed.

'You crazy galoot! You think I'd ride out here for a lousy two dollars. The note. I want the note.'

'What note?' Will started to look worried.

Clancy drew his pistol and cocked the hammer. 'You want remindin'?'

'Oh, that note, it's just a message for Doc Mayweather, is all,' Will started to feel around with his right hand for the shotgun he kept by the seat. He felt the wooden stock and slid his hand up to the double hammers. Silently, he pulled one back and felt for the trigger guard. Will might be treated as the town drunk and sometimes idiot, but he was no fool. He knew that whether he handed the note over or not, Clancy would kill him.

He wrapped his finger round the trigger, and moving faster than anyone would have believed, brought up the shotgun and fired.

Clancy had been too complacent, treating the old man as if he was a fool, and was taken completely by surprise. The speed the old man had moved with suddenly seemed to be in slow motion. Clancy was sure that, as the shotgun blasted, he could see the 12-bore shot flying towards him. His last act was instinctive, the pure reflex of a gunny. In that last second of his life, he squeezed the trigger of the .45 as the shotgun pellets peppered his head and chest, the force at such close range knocking him backwards, head over heels, to land with a sickening crunch in the dirt.

Clancy's .45 slug caught old Will on the forehead, blowing the top of his skull clean off. The force of the slug sent him reeling into the back of the buckboard.

Clancy's horse bolted, while the old nag pulling the buckboard merely stopped grazing and began to walk forwards. He knew the way home.

CHAPTER SIX

Mitch was the first to wake up. He pulled his Stetson off his eyes as he heard the creaking sound of wagon wheels and the jingling of harness. Rubbing the sleep from his eyes, he began to focus a little. Then he sat bolt upright, his gun already drawn as he looked at the empty buckboard slowly meandering down the trail towards Calvary.

Mitch stood, the gun aimed at the buckboard. 'Cal, Cal, wake up and cover me.'

Cal woke with a start – so deep had he slept that for a moment, he didn't even know where he was. His leg soon reminded him.

'What, what the . . .?' he stuttered.

'Cover me, Cal. There's an empty wagon on the trail. I'm gonna check it out, and I don't want any surprises.' He handed Cal a Winchester.

'Ready?' Mitch said.

'Ready,' Cal replied.

Coming more to his senses, Cal realized he recognized the buckboard and horse.

'Hold up, Mitch. That buckboard belongs to the

Palace saloon! I'm sure of it. Ol' Will Garrett uses it for delivery and collection for his boss.'

'Well, it sure looks empty now,' Mitch said. 'Just cover me while I check it out, OK?'

'OK.'

Slowly and keeping low, Mitch crept across the open land towards the trail. The nag pulling the buckboard seemed unconcerned as he made his way along the trail. Reaching the back of the buckboard, gun raised, Mitch stood and peered into the rear of the wagon – and nearly brought up his beans and coffee. It took him a few minutes to regain his composure, then he replaced his gun and ran to stop the horse, which seemed oblivious to everything except getting back to town.

Grabbing the reins, Mitch pulled the nag to one side of the trail and ground hitched it, the animal quite content to graze on the lusher grass.

'What is it, Mitch?' Cal called out as he saw Mitch lean on the side of the wagon, take his hat off and wipe his head with a bandanna.

'Dead man,' was all he said.

'Let me see,' Call called out, 'git me on my horse.'

Once astride his horse, Cal rode to the wagon and peered inside.

'Geez! You could'a warned me!' Cal said, his horse skittering and snorting as the smell of blood filled its nostrils.

'Steady boy,' Cal said, stroking the animal's neck.

'You recognize him? Or what's left of him?' Mitch asked.

Cal stared as if transfixed at the crumpled form of

46

what used to be Will Garrett. With the top of his head missing and the wagon soaked in blood it was still easy to tell who it was. The bed of the wagon was a seething mass of flies and the stench of death overpowering.

'That's Will, all right,' Cal said, covering his mouth and nose with his bandanna. 'Only two places he could have come from.'

Mitch gritted his teeth. 'Sure as eggs is eggs, it weren't from Brad's place.'

'We better get him buried afore buzzards start having a go,' Cal said. 'Poor critter didn't deserve this.'

'There's a spade attached to the side of the wagon. I'll start digging, ain't no way you can,' Mitch said, and dismounted.

Maria knew, without a shadow of a doubt, that her note would never reach Doc Mayweather. Her last hope of contacting anyone was sure to fail now, and she would be at the mercy of Latham Parry. She was under siege, and she knew it. Her first priority was to protect Josh at all costs – including with her own life – so the first thing to do was to make sure the ranch house was as impregnable as she could manage.

When Josh had designed and built the ranch house many years ago, no expense had been spared. There was always a constant danger of Indian attack in those days, and Josh had ensured that his home would be as safe as he could make it. Every window was barred, and the front door and two rear doors were all equipped with double locks and a sturdy wooden cross-bar. There was a large root cellar under the kitchen, and a tunnel that ran for a hundred yards away from the house. To that day, only he and Maria knew about the secret tunnel.

Even the roof was safe: wood was the conventional covering, but Josh had used imported slate tiles that were impervious to the flaming arrows of any Indian attack.

Maria locked and barred the front door, then did the same with the two back doors. She climbed the stairs to Josh's room, and entered the darkened bedroom silently.

She wasn't sure if Josh was asleep or unconscious. His breathing was shallow, and every time he breathed in there was a rattling sound. To Maria, it sounded like death was very near.

She leaned closer and kissed him gently on the cheek and dipped a cloth into a bowl of iced water to mop his brow.

As Maria stared at his ashen face, a small smile seemed to escape his lips. Josh Winters breathed in, then out, in a slow, laborious way. The man was fighting to stay alive.

In the sweltering heat, it took Mitch over an hour of hard digging before he had a hole deep enough to bury Will Garrett.

He hoped it was deep enough to prevent critters from digging him up.

Grabbing hold of Will's booted legs, he unceremoniously dragged him off the flatbed. There was no way he could lift him as his shoulder was still stiff and painful, but more than that, the top half of Will's body was soaked in blood and being feasted on by flies.

'Sorry, old timer,' Mitch said under his breath. 'But there ain't no way I can lift you.'

As the body hit the dirt, a scrap of paper fell from Will's vest pocket. Mitch lowered the dead man's legs and picked up the piece of paper.

'What ya got there?' Cal asked.

Mitch didn't reply straightaway – he was reading the note.

'What is it, Mitch?' Cal asked again.

'Seems ol' Josh Winters is dying, an' this woman . . . er . . .' he paused as he skimmed down the note to Maria's name, '. . . Maria, thinks there's something bad going on.'

'If Winters is dyin', then Parry must be up to something,' Cal said.

'He reckon on takin' over the Bar-Q?' Mitch asked.

'I reckon he wants to take over the whole valley,' Cal said.

'Makes sense,' Mitch said. 'The telegram I got from my brother told me he had steers missing, coupl'a dozen at a time. Said he was having trouble with a neighbouring ranch, but didn't say who.'

'Only one it could be,' Cal said.

'I'll finish up here,' Mitch said, grabbing hold of Will's legs once more. 'Then we'll ride to the Bar-B.'

Mitch laid Will to rest as gently as he could in the grave and began covering him up. There were no rocks to cover the grave, so Mitch tramped the bare earth down as much as he could and hoped Will would rest in peace. He stood for a moment, his head bowed, leaning on the shovel; then wiping his brow, he grabbed his Stetson and turned to Cal.

'You might find it easier to drive the wagon. At least

you can stretch out your leg a-whiles.'

'I'll try it,' Cal said, 'if'n you could give me a hand.'

'Sure thing,' Mitch said.

Mitch helped Cal into the driver's seat of the buckboard.

'Hey,' Cal said, 'there's a shotgun here under the seat.' He lifted it up, and the smell of cordite was strong. 'Been fired recently, too.'

Cal broke the stock and checked the empty cases. 'Both barrels, too!'

'Well, at least he put up a fight,' Mitch said.

Mitch's thoughts turned to his brother and his family. His chest tightened as imaginary scenarios raced through his brain. Getting to the Bar-B became even more urgent.

The riderless horse cantered into the Bar-Q compound and walked straight to the trough. Drinking its fill, it then walked calmly to the barn and the hay it knew was waiting there. Some thirty minutes later a cowhand roughly shook Latham Parry awake in the bunkhouse.

'Boss, boss, wake up . . .'

Parry sat bolt upright, his Colt in his hand. 'What the hell . . .' He blinked, and his senses came alive.

'It's Clancy, boss,' the ranch hand said.

Parry rubbed his face. 'What about him?'

'He ain't come back, boss.'

'You woke me up to tell me that?' Parry was almost incandescent.

'His horse is back, but he ain't on it,' said the hand in a shaky voice. This woke up Latham Parry quicker than a bucket of cold water. His mind was racing now. No way could that old drunk outgun Clancy, no way.

'Get some boys together, we're ridin' out!'

'Sure thing, boss.' The man hurried off, thankful for his life.

In less than ten minutes, Latham Parry led four men out of the ranch and along the trail to Calvary; Parry knew they wouldn't need to ride that far. Twenty minutes later they found Clancy – or rather, what was left of him. A dozen buzzards scattered at the riders approached, the sound of their flapping wings and raucous screeches filling the air as they rose skywards, angry at being disturbed.

Parry reined in and dismounted, and stood over the remains of Clancy. Strong as his stomach was, Parry had to fight to keep the bile down. Clancy was almost unrecognizable facially. His eyes were gone, as was most of the soft flesh around them, and the lips had disappeared, making him look like a grinning skull. His shirt was ripped open and blood-soaked. Parry could see ribs showing where the buzzards had feasted, and flies were swarming now the birds had disappeared.

The four hands sat silently on their mounts until one asked, 'That Clancy, boss?'

Parry nodded. 'Can't tell from his face, but look at his boots.'

Clancy's liking for hand-tooled boots was well known, especially the two-tone ones they could see now.

'Shall I go fetch a wagon, Boss?' one of the men asked.

Parry nodded again. 'Yeah, we can't leave him here.'

The man wheeled his horse around and set off at a

gallop back to the ranch, glad to get away. Parry lit a cheroot and inhaled deeply. Right now he wished he had a bottle of whiskey. He started to inspect the ground around the body. Most of it was chewed up by the fighting buzzards, but on the trail he saw the wheelmarks of a wagon. And blood!

So, Parry thought, Clancy didn't go down without a fight! And there was a faint trail of blood leading away from the death scene. So was Will dead, or merely wounded?

One way or another, Parry knew he had to find out. If Will had made it to Calvary he knew his plans could be thwarted. It wouldn't take long for the law to become involved, and that would complicate matters considerably. He looked at the three rannies, nervously sitting their mounts, and wondered which one he could trust the most. Clancy had been his right-hand man. Now he was gone.

Parry made up his mind. Burt Haystack – although Parry was sure that wasn't his real name – stood around six feet eight inches tall, a giant of a man, pretty handy with a gun and deadly with his fists.

'Burt, here a minute.'

Burt edged his horse over to Parry and dismounted. 'Boss?'

'I need a man I can trust. Can I trust you?' Parry asked.

'Do I get paid extra?' Burt said.

'As deputy foreman, yes.'

'Then you can trust me,' Burt said, and smiled, showing tobacco-stained teeth.

Parry looked up into the big man's eyes, and lowering

his voice, told him about the note.

'I need you to ride into Calvary and keep your ears and eyes open. I have to know if Will made it there or not.'

'An' if he did?' Burt asked, knowing the answer.

'If he did, he's wounded an' there's only one doc in town. Chances are, Will would have passed the note to him. There ain't no law in Calvary, no telegraph office either, and the nearest sheriff is a two-day ride away. Should be easy to make sure that note don't go no further.'

'I get the message,' Burt replied, and mounting up, said, 'I'll report back in a few hours, boss.'

Parry watched him go and thought, well, at least the man has savvy. Then he mounted up himself and ordered the remaining two rannies to wait for the buckboard and get Clancy back to the ranch. They'd bury him there.

Maria had busied herself in the house. There was never much housework needed, except for perpetual dusting, and she was able to keep her eye on the approach to the ranch. She heated up a beef stew she'd made the day before and prepared to feed Josh. Or at least, try to.

Placing the bowl on a tray, she climbed the stairs and entered the darkened bedroom.

Josh was still asleep, so she gently placed the tray on a small table and opened the thick drapes to let the sunlight in.

She watched as the buckboard came hurtling out of the barn. Immediately she knew that something serious had happened. She sighed, knowing that pretty soon all hell could break loose. She just wished she knew what!

She moved across the room to Josh's bed and began to mop his brow once more. His face was grey and he felt cold to the touch, but beads of sweat formed on his forehead. His breathing was much shallower than earlier, every breath an effort.

Josh's eyes flickered open. Maria saw they were a dull, almost lifeless grey. For a few seconds it seemed that Josh was confused, unsure of where he was. Then, slowly, that smile of his appeared on his face, and briefly, his eyes sparkled.

Maria smiled back, hiding her fears and concern. 'I have some soup,' she said. 'If you can manage it.'

Josh shook his head. He reached for her hand and gripped it firmly, and gave it a gentle squeeze.

Mitch and Cal reached the fork in the trail. Straight ahead was the Bar-Q, while the trail to the left led to the Bar-B.

'How far now, Cal?' Mitch asked.

'No more'n five miles,' he replied.

'Be good to get out of this heat,' Mitch said. 'A cool glass of lemonade wouldn't go amiss either.'

'I could do with a beer,' Cal grinned.

The land either side of the trail was lush grassland for as far as the eye could see. Here and there, small clumps of cottonwoods added to the beauty of the land, and a clear blue sky made the perfect backdrop. The whole scene almost took Mitch's breath away. He rolled a cigarette as he walked his horse onwards, and he felt at peace with the world.

Soon they reached an ornately carved wooden arch

bearing the name of the ranch – and almost at the same time, Mitch caught the smell of smoke. At first he assumed the stove had been lit, but then in the distance he saw a thin spiral of white smoke hanging lazily in the air.

Mitch suddenly lost interest in his cigarette and flicked it away.

'Follow on, Cal, I'm gonna check out that smoke,' he said, concern evident in his voice.

Without waiting for a reply, Mitch spurred his horse into a gallop. As he neared the still smouldering building he reined in, and with a sense of foreboding, walked the horse forwards slowly.

The house had burned to the ground; the only part of it still standing was the stone chimney stack.

'Jesus!' Mitch muttered under his breath as he walked toward the ruin.

Then he stopped in his tracks.

Lying on the ground at his feet were the charred remains of what used to be a human being. It was lying face down, arms outstretched, the hands mere stumps with the fingers burned off.

Mitch was violently sick. The sight and the smell of burnt flesh lingered in the air and it was more than he could take.

He fell to his knees. He was sure the body that lay before him was his brother.

Taking a deep breath, he filled his lungs with air in an effort not to be sick again. He needed to turn the body over to confirm his suspicions. Getting to his feet he reached inside his saddlebags and brought out a pair of gloves. Kneeling once more, he grabbed hold of an arm and pulled. To his disgust, the arm came away from the body, and for a second or two, Mitch could neither move nor let go of it.

Then he flung it from him as if it were still on fire.

At that moment Cal arrived. Shock was written all over his face as he saw the arm fly through the air.

'What the hell? Is that . . .?' He stopped, knowing the answer to his own question.

'I need to make sure,' Mitch said, his voice quivering.

Placing one hand under the chest and the other by the hips, he turned the body over as gently as he could.

The front of the body wasn't as badly burned as the back – Mitch guessed the ground had stopped most of the burning. He saw the watch chain straightaway, and pulling it, he revealed a Hunter pocket watch – the one their father had given Brad.

Mitch stood, head bowed as he stared at the watch in the palm of his hand.

Cal got himself down off the buckboard and grabbed the crutch Doc Mayweather had given him. He stood beside Mitch, unsure of what to say, so he said nothing.

Suddenly, Mitch started towards the smoking embers of the house, shouting at the top of his voice:

'Julia, Julia!'

As fast as he could, Cal limped back to the wagon and grabbed the shovel. He couldn't think of anything else to do.

Mitch stood and stared at the remains of the small ranch house, fighting back tears.

'Maybe his wife . . .' Cal began.

'She's either dead, or the Indians took her,' Mitch said, finding it hard to control the tremor in his voice.

'Indians? There ain't been Indians round here for months,' Cal said.

Mitch pointed. 'There's arrows in the dirt, the ones that missed the house.'

Cal walked towards the nearest arrow and pulled it out of the ground. He studied it for a few moments and said, 'This ain't no Indian arrow. I seen these before.'

'What?'

'Parry figured we were wasting too many slugs shooting at cans and such, so we set up a target and shot arrows. These arrows, I recognize the feathers.'

Anger began to well up in Mitch as this information sank in. He grabbed the shovel and strode into the smouldering embers. He had to find out if Julia and baby Jon were in there someplace.

'I'll check the outbuildings,' Cal said. He didn't want to be around if Brad's wife and child were found burned to death.

Burt Haystack cantered down the trail. The tracks were easy to follow, as the wagon wheels had left deep ruts in the sand. But as he reached the fork he reined in and scratched his head.

'What the hell?' he thought.

The signs he was following continued on towards Calvary, but there were fresher tracks that came back towards him and took the trail to the Bar-B. So did the old man change his mind? Burt had been with Parry when they torched the ranch house, so if the old man had gone there, there would be no help for his wound – if indeed he was wounded.

Haystack was a slow thinker. Should he ride back to the Bar-Q and report to Parry? Or ride down towards the Bar-B?

He dismounted and checked the signs more thoroughly. This time he could tell there were three horses: the nag that pulled the buckboard, easy to spot because one of its hoofs had recently lost a shoe, and two others, and judging by the depth of the hoofmarks, one was mounted, the other not.

Haystack's brain was turning over laboriously as he tried to decide what to do. If he went back empty-handed and with no idea whether the old man was alive or dead, Parry would go mad. Haystack wasn't exactly afraid of Parry – in a straight fight, Haystack had no match in the art of fisticuffs. But he knew Parry wasn't a fair man, and he'd seen him use those twin Colts he always wore, so it would never be a fair fight, man to man. On the other hand, if he rode the trail to the Bar-B he might find out what was going on – or be shot dead for trying. He was stuck between a rock and a hard place.

But maybe, he thought, there was a third alternative?

A slow thinker he might be, but Haystack was no fool. He decided to follow the wagon's tracks towards Calvary. That way, he reasoned, he could find out where, and maybe why, the buckboard had done a U-turn.

With his mind eventually made up, Haystack mounted up and set off down the trail.

CHAPTER SEVEN

Latham Parry was becoming more and more agitated as the time ticked slowly by. And the more agitated he became, the more his anger built up. He paced back and forth inside the bunkhouse, and the men not out on the prairie gave him a wide berth. Each man knew that Parry could vent out his anger on any one of them for no reason at all.

Parry lit yet another cigarette and then poured coffee into his tin mug, but spat it out. The brew had become stewed and the bitter taste only added to his anger. He grabbed hold of the coffee pot and flung it across the room where it crashed into the wall, splattering coffee everywhere.

He stormed outside and bellowed, 'Beefsteak, git in here and sort this mess out!'

Beefsteak, who doubled as camp cook and odd-job man, left the corral fence he was mending and made his way to the bunkhouse; he avoided looking directly at Parry for fear of annoying the man even more.

'And git some fresh coffee on, that stuff ain't fit for a

coyote to drink.'

'Yes sir, right away boss,' Beefsteak mumbled, and entered the bunkhouse. He retrieved the coffee pot, but couldn't find the lid. Easing his old bones down on to the floor, he got on all fours and crawled around, peering under the bunks until he found the lid. Parry was still outside and every single man in and around the corral and barn area made themselves scarce.

'There ain't no sign of any . . .' Cal stopped; he didn't want to say 'bodies'.

'I'll check the barn,' Mitch said and ran across the small compound; more in hope than certainty, he entered, but he already knew they wouldn't be there.

Slowly he made his way back to the burned-out ranch house and stood beside Cal.

'Mitch, no one could have survived this fire,' Cal placed a hand on Mitch's shoulder.

'So where are the remains?' Mitch said. 'There must be something!'

Mitch started to walk through the ash, kicking it up as he went, searching for any trace of his sister-in-law and nephew. Then suddenly, Mitch disappeared. It was missed by Cal, who was scanning the skyline. When he turned back, there was no Mitch to be seen.

'Mitch? Mitch? Where are you?' Cal called out.

There was no reply.

Burt Haystack had set his mount into a trot, following the wheeltracks towards Calvary, when he reined in. He'd reached the point of the trail where the buckboard had stopped and the two unknown riders had met it.

Burt dismounted and studied the ground. Dried red and black stains were visible on the soft sand, and to his left, he saw where something bloody had been dragged through it; drawing his gun, he followed the path. It stopped abruptly at a rectangle of freshly dug soil.

Studying the surrounding area, Burt saw that, to one side of the grave, where soil had been piled prior to filling in the hole, there were two sets of boot prints – and something else: small round circles that were deeper than the boot prints. Burt's slow-moving brain began to work out the sequence of events, and he breathed a sigh of relief. He had something definite to tell Parry.

He grabbed his canteen and took a few swigs – it wasn't exactly filled with water: contrary to ranch rules, it contained only whiskey. Without it, Haystack couldn't function. He replaced the stopper and hung the canteen on the cantle, and mounted up. Spurring his horse, he set off back to the Bar-Q.

Summoning up all his energy, and filled with a sense of panic and foreboding, Cal, too, stepped into the charred remains of the ranch house.

'Mitch?' he called out again, but there was still no reply.

Then he saw it: a gaping black hole in the centre of the rubble. He looked down, but it was pitch black, puffs of smoke rose lazily into the air.

'Mitch, goddammit! You hear me?'

There was a low groan and Cal thought he saw movement. 'Mitch, you OK?'

A stunned Mitch sat up and rubbed the back of his head. It took him a few minutes to orientate himself. He shook his head and said, 'Yeah, I'm OK.'

Relief flooded through Cal's body. 'I'll get rope, soon have you outa there,' Cal said.

Mitch struck a match – and then he saw them: huddled in a corner, the baby still clasped in her arms, sat Julia, her eyes closed. She looked serene, almost as if she was taking a short sleep, but Mitch knew she was dead, as was baby Jon. A thousand thoughts rushed through Mitch's brain as he stared in horror. Brad must have sent them down here to keep them safe, but he hadn't figured on the smoke!

The match burned down and Mitch felt the pain as it burned his fingers. He struck another and crawled across the floor of the root cellar. He had to make sure. Just in case.

His shoulder was throbbing again; he thought he must have landed on it in his fall. He felt a warm sensation on his arm and knew the wound had opened up. Ignoring the pain, he reached Julia's side, blew out the match, and struck another. Placing his fingers on her neck, he felt for a pulse. His head sank on to his chest and an involuntary sob escaped his mouth as he felt nothing. Just cool skin on a slender neck.

He was too late. Too late to help his brother, too late to help his wife and child.

Anger surged through his body. Initially at Cal. If he hadn't delayed him, Mitch knew he could have helped Brad. Then at the unknown Latham Parry, who, he knew instinctively, was behind this.

'I got a rope, Mitch,' Cal called down.

'Forget it,' Mitch said through gritted teeth, trying to get his voice even. 'There's a ladder down here.'

'Are they, are they down there?' Cal asked tentatively.

'Yeah. Yeah, they're down here.'

'Are they . . .?'

'Stop asking dumb questions. They're both dead, OK?' Mitch's anger was too strong to contain.

Cal took a step back from the cellar door and drew in his breath sharply. He knew he was partly responsible for what had happened – if only he . . .

Mitch's head appeared from the root cellar, but Cal couldn't look him in the eye.

'I'm sorry, Mitch. This is all my fault,' Cal managed to say.

Mitch didn't reply straightaway. He climbed out of the hole, brushed himself down, and was at a loss as what to do.

He looked at Cal. The man was genuinely upset and for all his anger, Mitch couldn't really blame him.

'I wouldn't blame you for killin' me right now,' Cal said.

'I ain't gonna kill ya,' Mitch said, and walked over to his horse; he grabbed his canteen, took mighty gulps, then poured the remaining water over his head.

'We need to get them on to the wagon and into town,' Mitch said, more to himself than Cal. 'There's some horse blankets in the barn.'

'I'll get 'em,' Cal said, glad to be doing something.

Mitch lit a cigarette and inhaled deeply, noticing how much his hand shook as he brought the cigarette to his lips. It took five minutes for Cal to return, carrying the blankets.

'I'll bring them up,' was all Mitch said, and he climbed down the ladder. 'Spread the blanket out on the open ground,' he ordered.

Cal did as he was told. Within a few moments, Mitch had prised the baby from his mother's arms and carried him up the ladder.

'Here, take baby Jon. Gently!'

Cal took the small bundle, and a tear coursed down his cheek as he laid the baby on the blanket and covered up the little body.

Julia took a mite longer. In the cool root cellar, rigor mortis had set in, so Mitch had to carry her cradled in his arms, which made it difficult to climb the ladder.

'Can you reach down, Cal?' Mitch called out.

'Sure.' Cal dropped his crutch and knelt on his good knee and placed his hands under Julia's arms. Taking her weight from Mitch momentarily, Mitch was able to push her up and clear of the root cellar.

He took her body from Cal and laid her down on a blanket. Taking one last look, he covered her up and they lifted her on to the buckboard. Cal brought the baby over and together they laid him by his mother. Neither man was looking forward to their next task: Brad.

They walked over to the remains of Brad Evans and stared once more in horror at the blackened frame. Mitch laid the blanket next to the body, then walked over to where he had tossed the arm, picked it up and placed it beside the blanket.

'I reckon we try and roll him on to the blanket,' Mitch

said. 'I ain't sure he'd stay in one piece if we try and lift him. You hold his legs and I'll take the head and torso,' Mitch added.

'OK? On the count of three: one, two, three!'

Together, the men rolled the body on to the blanket without losing any more limbs. Mitch placed the arm beside his brother and quickly covered him up. Again, Mitch took the head and torso and Cal the legs, and they gently lifted the body from the ground. It was surprisingly light.

With all three bodies now on the buckboard, Cal retrieved his crutch and scrambled on to the driver's seat.

'Let's move,' Mitch said.

He'd deal with Latham Parry when his family had been laid to rest in Calvary.

Burt Haystack was feeling pretty pleased with himself as he set his horse into a gentle trot. So pleased was he that he reached behind him and grabbed the canteen from the cantle. Another little nip would do no harm – besides, he deserved it. He slowed the horse to a walk, pulled the stopper out with his teeth and raised the canteen to his lips. He felt the liquid slide down his throat and hit his stomach with a slight burning sensation. It wasn't the best quality whiskey, but it wasn't the cheap stuff either.

The feeling was good, and despite the heat of the late afternoon, he began to feel the warm glow creep through his body. Then without warning, his horse suddenly stumbled – one of its front hoofs sank into a small hole on the trail, and it lurched to one side. This caught Haystack unprepared; he was only loosely holding the reins with one hand, with the canteen pressed to his lips with the other, and he tumbled forwards and somersaulted over the animal's neck, landing heavily on the ground. With the wind knocked out of him, Haystack stayed where he was, fighting to get his breath back. But he still held the canteen, and hadn't spilled a drop!

Gradually, his breathing became easier and he sat up. His first thought was to put the stopper back on the canteen, but then he took another slug. He looked at his horse, hoping it hadn't broken a leg. It was standing quite calmly beside the trail, grazing and seemingly unhurt. Hauling himself to his feet, Haystack staggered and lurched on his feet, only just regaining his balance. He'd drunk more than he intended, but it felt good and he grinned stupidly to himself.

'Ol' Parry won't like that. No siree! Won't like that one bit,' he said out loud, and staggered sideways. He giggled again as he reached for the reins. Big as he was, Haystack had his Achilles heel, and it was contained in his canteen.

After three unsuccessful attempts at getting his foot into the stirrup, he succeeded at the fourth and hefted his huge bulk into the saddle. Swaying slightly, he spurred the animal on.

Having fed and watered the horses, Mitch and Cal set off for Calvary. The late afternoon sun still beat down, and the heat from the ground rose in gentle spirals, mirages dancing before their eyes as they headed for the fork in the trail. They reached it without incident, Mitch keeping an eye on their gruesome cargo, his thoughts whirling as he remembered his dead brother and family.

It was Cal who noticed the fresh tracks. One horse, and it was carrying a heavy load, judging by the depth of the hoofprints.

'Mitch,' Cal called out. 'Seems there's been a lone horseman down here recently.'

Mitch was brought back to reality: 'Huh?'

'Look yonder,' Cal said.

Mitch saw the tracks, but dismissed them as he saw in the distance a dust cloud, and it was coming their way.

'Seems there's someone coming this way,' Mitch said, pointing.

Cal reined in and peered ahead, but the figure was too distant to make out who it might be.

'Sure as eggs is eggs it's a Bar-Q rider,' Cal said, and picked up the Winchester and cocked it. He placed it across his lap in readiness.

Mitch reached into his saddlebag and brought out an old army telescope. Through it he could make out the features of the rider.

'Sure is a big fella,' he said, and handed the 'scope to Cal.

Cal grunted. 'Damn!' he said.

'Recognize him?' Mitch asked.

'Yeah. It's Burt Haystack, one of Parry's henchmen.'

'He's on a recce, sure enough,' Mitch said as he took the 'scope back. 'Parry must want this note real bad.'

'Whatever he's planning started with your brother and his family,' Cal said. 'He must be getting ready to take over the Bar-Q, an' if ol' man Winters is on his last legs, Parry won't want any outsiders interfering.'

Mitch put the spyglass to his eye once more and peered at the oncoming rider.

'He's taken out his rifle,' Mitch said. 'Get down behind the footboard, Cal.'

A shot rang out, and fortunately for the two men, Haystack was as good with a rifle as he was with a Colt, his aim so wide that Mitch didn't even hear the bullet. Mitch jumped to the ground as Cal took hold of his Winchester, and they both returned fire.

Haystack dismounted as quickly as his huge frame would allow and landed heavily in the hard-packed sand of the trail. Lying flat on his stomach, Haystack sighted down the barrel of his rifle and started shooting again, though his aim was no better than it had been before. The distance between him and the buckboard was no more than a hundred yards, well within range of the Winchester, but Haystack couldn't get a shot anywhere near, overshooting, undershooting and wild wide shots.

'Hold fire, Cal,' Mitch shouted, 'he couldn't hit the side of a barn from ten paces.'

'We can't stay here for ever,' Cal said.

'Cover me, Cal. I'm gonna make my way over yonder' – he pointed to his right – 'we might catch him in cross-fire.'

'OK. But keep low, he's a lousy shot but he might get a lucky one in,' Cal said.

'Lucky? Sure wouldn't be lucky for me,' Mitch said, and started towards the tall grassland to the right of the trail. Once off the trail, he was completely hidden by the grass – all Cal could see was the grass moving as Mitch made his way towards Haystack.

He began firing at Haystack again, keeping the man low on the ground. There was no return fire. Even Haystack realized he had no chance of hitting anyone. Using the covering fire, Mitch made a wide arc through the grass until he felt he was somewhere to the right of Haystack; then stooping, he raised his head high enough to get a clear view.

His guess had been a good one: he was no more than fifteen feet away. Now he had his bearings he ducked down. Cal had lost sight of Mitch, but he made sporadic shots to keep Haystack busy. Mitch decided to talk first, and shoot only if necessary.

'Throw down your weapons, Haystack, and stand up real slow with your hands in the air where I can see them.'

Silence.

'One last chance, Haystack,' Mitch yelled.

Then Mitch heard the distinctive sound of a rifle being cocked, ready to shoot.

'Give it up, man. I've no wish to kill you, but I will if you try anything.' Mitch waited.

He didn't have to wait long. A slug hissed past his left ear and he dived to the ground. Chambering his Winchester, he waited for Cal to provide covering fire, and when he did, he jumped up and loosed off two quick shots. After the second, he heard a deep grunt.

Mitch cocked the rifle for a third time but held his fire. The eerie silence was only broken by the warm breeze rustling the tall grass.

'You see anything, Cal?' Mitch called out.

'Nope, he ain't moving,' Cal responded.

Mitch tentatively got to his haunches, rifle ready, then raised his head above the grass. He could see Haystack clearly – and the blood. Mitch stood up and walked the short distance to the giant man's body, his rifle hanging loosely by his side.

Blood was oozing from the right side of Haystack's stomach. There were two wounds, so Mitch knew that both his shots had found their target. Flies were already beginning to start buzzing around the pool of dark blood, and Mitch used his Stetson to swat at them. Then he heard a groan. So the man was still alive – barely – but alive.

Mitch waved to Cal, beckoning him to bring the buckboard down. Within minutes, Cal drew up in a cloud of choking dust.

'Goddammit, Cal!' Mitch said, coughing and pulling up his bandanna over his nose.

Cal ignored the remark, and both men waited for the dust to settle.

'He ain't dead yet,' Mitch said. Cal clambered off the wagon stood beside the body of Burt Haystack. 'Hell,' Cal said. 'What're we gonna do?'

'Beats me,' Mitch said. 'I ain't no doc, and there's no way we can load him on the wagon.'

'We'll have to leave him here,' Cal said. 'We ain't got no choice.'

'We can't do that,' Mitch said.

'What d'you suggest, then? It'd take four or five men to lift that hulk off the ground, and I got only one good leg an' you got only one arm.'

Without replying, Mitch walked over to Haystack's

mount and gave it a mighty whack on the rump. The startled animal, which was content to munch on the grass and was grateful not to have its giant master on its back, set off at a frenzied gallop.

'What the hell?' Cal started.

'If his horse gets back to the Bar-Q riderless, they'll send a hunting party out to investigate,' Mitch said. 'That way, I figure we can leave him here.'

'Let's git outa here,' Cal said, and mounted the buckboard. Mitch could see he was moving a lot easier now, and mounted up himself.

'Let's go,' he said, and they set off for Calvary in silence.

Latham Parry had his trusty band of men alone in the bunkhouse. He was getting impatient, waiting for Burt Haystack to return. He had to know what was going on and what was in that note.

His first thoughts were to rush the ranch house and force Maria to tell him, but he knew she'd die before she betrayed the old man. No, he'd have to wait. But he wouldn't wait long.

CHAPTER EIGHT

Maria was beside herself with worry. Josh Winters was more unconscious than asleep and she needed the doctor out here as soon as possible.

The ranch house was practically impregnable – Josh had seen to that in the early days – and the only way anyone could get in was with an axe through one of the walls, and that seemed unlikely. There was a plentiful supply of food in the root cellar beneath the kitchen, and salt beef in abundance; also the kitchen had its own water pump, so in a siege situation she knew she could hold out until help came.

She also knew that Josh couldn't. She gently lifted the old man's head and plumped up the pillows before lowering him down again. Then as she bathed his forehead with cold water, noises out in the courtyard caught her attention. She moved to the window and pulled one of the drapes slightly apart, and peered out through the barred window. It was late afternoon and the shadows were lengthening, thin fingers of black seeming to devour the land near the western horizon.

In the courtyard she could see six or seven men clustered round a horse. She had no idea who the horse belonged to, but there seemed to be a lot of animated conversation going on – most of it coming from the ranch foreman, Latham Parry. The ranch house was at least two hundred yards from the barn, and at that distance it was impossible to hear what was being said, but whatever it was, it wasn't good news.

Parry was all but stamping his feet like a spoilt child, and the ranch hands were visibly drawing back from him. It seemed as though he was barking out orders, as suddenly, two men ran towards the barn, and five minutes later thundered out and hit the trail to town. Parry slapped his thigh with his crumpled derby and led the horse into the stables.

Maria quietly closed the drapes and wondered what on earth was going on. She was certain it had something to do with Will Garrett and the note she thought she had surreptitiously passed to him. If Parry got that note...!

Maria silently slipped out of Josh's bedroom and made her way down to the study. There, she sorted through her keys and found the one she was looking for. She unlocked the gun cabinet and stood back.

There were four of the latest Winchester rifles and a Sharps, all fixed upright side by side. On one shelf was a selection of handguns, mostly Colts, and below that, another shelf stacked with boxes of ammunition. At the base of the cabinet was a drawer with two heavy brass handles. Maria slid the drawer open and removed an ornately hand-tooled holster.

She removed it and smiled at the memories it brought

back, as the smell of the leather filled her nostrils. Josh had bought them for her and insisted she learn to use both a handgun and a rifle. With the gun belt he'd also purchased a pearl-handled Colt and silver-plated Winchester, both .45 calibre. It hadn't taken Josh long to discover that she was a natural – not a fast draw, but extremely accurate, and she could outshoot him with her eyes shut.

The gun belt had been made especially to fit her slim waist, and she slipped it on, then loaded her Colt and holstered it. She hadn't worn the gun rig for a good few years and she was aware of the weight on her hips.

She then took hold of the silver-plated Winchester and loaded that, too. She took out four boxes of ammunition, two hundred bullets – which she thought was a bit excessive, but better safe than sorry – and carried them through to the kitchen. Pouring herself a coffee, she sat at the kitchen table and waited.

Mitch and Cal could see the lights of Calvary in the distance. Early evening dusk was beginning to fall, but Cal knew they'd reach town before it got dark. Mitch had been silent since the incident with Haystack, his thoughts now on his brother, sister-in-law and his nephew. He was also pondering the note he had in his vest pocket. He had no proof, except Cal's confession and the arrow, that Latham Parry was behind this, but his gut reaction told him the man was evil and needed to be stopped. The question was, how?

There was no law in Calvary, the nearest peace officer was over a hundred miles to the east, and the chances of a US marshal passing through town seemed pretty remote. He was so deep in thought that he failed to hear the thunder of hoofs approaching rapidly from the rear. But he heard the gunshot, and the slug that thudded into the back of the buckboard.

'Shee-it!' Cal yelled. 'I guess they found Haystack!'

'Looks that way,' Mitch said, pulling out his rifle and jumping to the ground. 'We can't outrun 'em, Cal. Keep low and commence to shootin'.'

So saying, the two men set off a volley of shots. In the distance they could see two riders, who immediately reined in, sending up a cloud of dust that obscured the view of all four men. Then, silence.

'You see 'em, Cal?' Mitch called out.

'Too much dust, wait till it settles,' Cal replied.

Two more shots rang out, too close for comfort.

Mitch saw the flashes as the rifles were fired. 'They've split up Cal,' he called. 'You take the one on the left, I'll take the right.'

'OK,' Cal said, and concentrated his vision to the left of the trail. The grassland here was much shorter so cover was harder to find.

Another shot rang out and Mitch aimed at the gun flash. Immediately he heard a deep groan. Whoever was out there had been hit, that was for sure. Mitch began to belly-crawl to the left of the trail to see if he could do the same with the second bushwhacker.

Cal was firing blindly – the light was fading as the sun sank ever deeper. A red glow, blood-like, bathed the scene as Mitch sighted down the rifle's barrel, looking for any sign of movement – and his patience was rewarded.

Slightly to his left he saw the gun flash, as did Cal, and both men fired almost simultaneously. Then they waited, but there was no return fire.

'Cover me, Cal,' Mitch almost whispered. He got to his knees and peered ahead. He could see no movement, but he did see a dull red glow on the ground as the dying rays of the sun reflected off something metallic. Mitch crawled forwards until he could see the owner of the rifle. The man didn't move. Mitch waited a few moments, then keeping low, walked towards the body.

The man lying on the ground didn't move a muscle, and Mitch could see blood on his shoulder. He was about to lower his rifle when the man swiftly brought up the Winchester he held in one hand, and prepared to fire. But he was too slow, as Mitch triggered off a single shot that took the top of his head off. Blood gushed like a fountain for a minute or two, and the body slumped back flat to the ground.

Cal had dropped to the ground and hobbled over to Mitch. 'You OK?' he asked.

'Yeah, almost had me fooled there, playing possum. Let's check the other guy.' Mitch, followed by Cal, walked towards the other body.

'Goddamn!' Mitch exclaimed. 'He's gone!'

The bullet from Mitch's Winchester had creased the skull of Jed Jones, the second rider – another half inch to the left and his brains would have been spattered over the prairie. He had lain unconscious for a few minutes, then had come to with the sound of gunfire filling his ears. In the murky half light he had looked across to where his partner should have been, but all he saw was a man walking, crouched low, with a rifle in his hands. Jed knew there was nothing he could do as two quick shots were fired.

The man with the rifle was standing upright now and Jed knew his partner was dead. If he didn't move soon, he'd be next. His cow pony was less than ten feet away, munching on the rich grass – it took more than a few gunshots to rattle him. Jed gave a low whistle and the horse's ears pricked up as he lifted his head and looked in his direction.

'Come here, you mangy ol' cur,' Jed whispered.

The horse ambled over as if it had all the time in the world. Jed checked the two men on the other side of the trail, but they were preoccupied. His partner was obviously dead or badly wounded – either way, there was nothing he could do. Jed grabbed the reins and as quietly as he could, walked the pony as far away as he felt was safe enough to mount up.

With the light failing quickly now, it was becoming increasingly hard to see the two men, but he sure as hell recognized one of them: Cal Morgan!

Jed swung into the saddle – his head was spinning and his vision was slightly blurred as he dug his heels into the horse's flanks, the soft sand and grass muffling the sound of its galloping hoofs. He knew the boss would want to know what had gone on.

Latham Parry could no longer control his anger. The news that Jed had brought back was worse than he feared. So the man he'd sent to kill Brad Evans's brother was now fighting on his side! Damn the man. Damn him to hell!

Seething, Parry told his men to saddle up.

'What about Haystack? We never made it to Calvary to get the doc,' Jed said, and immediately regretted opening his mouth.

'The hell with Haystack, he can take care of himself. We gotta stop that wagon reaching town.' Parry stormed off to the barn to get his horse.

'I ain't too happy with this,' Jed said. 'Burning down the Evans' place was bad enough, hell knows what he's up to next.'

'We're in too deep now,' one of the men said.

'Yeah, an' you know the boss will never let you ride outa here alive,' added another.

'We best saddle up, I guess,' Jed said, reluctantly.

'Better get Chow to patch up your head first. He's over to the cookhouse.'

'OK. Wait up for me,' Jed said and dragged himself off to the cookhouse.

Maria stood in the front parlour watching the scene in the courtyard. Again, she couldn't hear what was being said, but it was obvious by Latham Parry's antics that whatever he had planned, had failed again. Maybe Will Garret had made it to Calvary after all!

Her hope was renewed.

'We best get moving,' Cal said. 'If'n he gets back to the Bar-Q, Parry is bound to send out his gang: there's more men than we can handle alone.'

78

'Guess you're right,' Mitch replied. 'Let's go.'

They set off at a faster pace, the distant lights becoming brighter and brighter as they neared the town and the evening drew in. After only thirty minutes, they entered town. As usual it was quiet. Cal pulled the wagon to a halt outside Doc Mayweather's house and wearily dismounted. Mitch was already knocking on the doc's front door.

The door creaked open and a surprised Mayweather eyed his visitors. 'Didn't expect to see you boys back so soon,' he said. 'Come in, come in.'

Mitch stood his ground. 'Are there enough men in town you trust?' Mitch asked.

'Trust? Well, sure, but why?'

'I got four bodies in the wagon, Doc. My brother and his wife and child, and an old-timer name of Garrett.'

'My God! What on earth . . .?'

'There ain't time to explain it all, Doc. We need to get these bodies somewhere decent and get some men together, men who can use a gun.'

'I've a stretcher in the surgery, I'll get it now,' the doc said, and disappeared inside.

Mitch had no wish to reveal the bodies of his family, so keeping them covered, he and the doc carried them inside one by one. Will Garrett was the last, and the only one not covered up. When they'd finished the gruesome task, the doc said: 'Now give me some idea of what's going on.'

Mitch related his story, keeping it as short as possible, then fished in his vest pocket and handed the doc the note they'd found on Will Garrett's body.

Doctor Mayweather. Mr Josh is dying before my eyes. I beg you to come to the Bar-Q as soon as possible.

I fear there is something evil going on outside. I have secured the ranch house against any intrusion. Whatever is going on, Latham Parry is behind it.

Maria

Mitch showed Mayweather the arrow he had found at the Bar-B. 'Cal said this is an arrow that the Bar-Q hands use for target practice, to save on bullets.'

'I've heard that, too,' the doc agreed. 'Right, get that wagon off the street an' I'll go see our town mayor and we'll organize ourselves.'

'You have a mayor?' Cal's surprise was evident in his voice.

'We got a town council, too,' the doc replied.

The doc turned to leave, but Mitch grabbed his arm. 'I fear Parry and his boys might well be heading to town as we speak. We were attacked twice on the way here, and Parry is bound to want to know what that note said.'

'Then I shall hurry,' the doc said, alarm clear in his voice.

'I'll take the wagon to the saloon barn,' Cal said, 'and feed this mangy critter.'

'No!' Mitch almost shouted. 'Take the horse, but leave the wagon. We might need a barricade.'

'Good thinking,' Cal said, and began to unhitch the horse.

*

Latham Parry was a man possessed. He'd been patiently planning his takeover of the Bar-Q and surrounding areas for nearly three years, and he wasn't about to let a low-life ranny and saddlebum stop him.

It had taken him ten years to track down his brother Larry, and he had found a shell of man, more dead than alive, living in a disused line shack in the middle of nowhere. His brother's only contact with the outside world was a trapper who called in periodically with vitals and moonshine.

His mind had gone. It took three weeks for Latham to find out what had happened to his older brother, which had reduced him to this state. Latham listened to his brother's broken voice as he related the story of how he'd lost most of his right arm, shot at by a stranger he'd never met before. And all because he was trying to kiss a Mexican girl!

Larry had come very close to dying through loss of blood, but he was lucky. At the corner of the alleyway he had seen a sign saying SURGERY, and the old doc inside had fought hard and long to save his life. He managed to stop the bleeding, and after two weeks of constant care, Larry had recovered. Physically, at least. Mentally his head was filled with anger, hatred and thoughts of revenge.

It took three months for Larry to be fit enough to leave. The old doc wouldn't accept a penny in payment, saying he had learned more in this one case than he had in a lifetime of delivering babies and digging out bullets.

No one had witnessed the shooting, and no one knew who the stranger was, or indeed, who the Mexican girl was. The only clue Larry had was that he had heard the name 'Maria'. At least, he thought he had: as he lay on the ground, shock having set in at seeing his shattered arm, either he had actually heard the name, or he had imagined it. Either way, the name 'Maria' in Mexico was as common as flies on a steer. But it was all he had.

Now it was all Latham had. At the end of three weeks, his brother died peacefully in his sleep. And Latham had vowed to dedicate the rest of his life to get even with the man who had caused this.

CHAPTER NINE

Doc Mayweather was a very persuasive man. The mayor wanted to form a committee, of course, to discuss the situation. 'We have to be democratic,' he'd argued.

'You can be as democratic as you like, lying in your grave,' the doc answered. 'There's already been six killed, and I believe Mitch Evans is right in his summation. You've seen the note from Maria – you want to see the bodies those two boys brought into town?'

'No, no, of course not,' the mayor replied.

'Then let's get some men together – we let Parry get away with this, and this town is as good as doomed!' Doc waited for the mayor's response.

The mayor was sweating profusely; he reached into his jacket pocket and brought out a handkerchief. Taking off his derby, he mopped his brow. He replaced his derby, put the handkerchief back in his pocket, and coughed.

'Well, seeing as how you put it that way . . .'

'We don't have time to dillydally, Mr Mayor,' the doc added.

'OK, let's do this!' The words were firm even if the delivery was not.

*

Mitch was astonished when, some thirty minutes after the doc had left, he returned with a motley selection of some twenty men. All were armed, one with a flintlock that looked as if it had never been fired.

'We got two choices,' Mitch said. 'We ride out to the Bar-Q, and possibly meet up with Latham Parry and his cronies, or we wait here till they ride in. Cos sure as eggs is eggs, Parry ain't gonna let this go.'

'I reckon town is a better option,' Doc Mayweather suggested. 'Parry won't be expecting a welcoming committee, so we'll have the element of surprise.'

'I agree,' Mitch said. 'I figure Parry is after me and the doc, here. He's already killed my brother and his family, and Maria sent a note to the doc, so seems likely.'

'Parry doesn't know about the note, does he?' the mayor asked.

'He doesn't know what the note said,' Mitch replied, 'but he knows there is one. Seems to me he's planning to get rid of the surrounding ranches and take over the Bar-Q, unless we stop him here and now.'

There was no further argument, so Mitch spoke again.

'I reckon Parry will make the surgery his target, so we need a couple of men opposite, up on the roof. I want half of you men to spread out along the street, keeping well down and giving you a clear shot to the front of the surgery.

'The rest of you do the same at the rear. Parry is no fool, he won't ride in gung-ho. Me, the doc and Cal will be inside the surgery, so make sure your shots don't hit us, OK?'

Two of the younger men elected for the roof opposite, the rest – most aged over fifty, shopkeepers, a barber and the liveryman – formed two groups and took up position at the front and rear of the surgery. The streets were deserted – even the saloon had closed and locked its doors. The whole town was eerily silent.

Now they waited.

Parry called a halt as they neared the scene of frantic buzzards fighting over a body in the dying rays of the sun.

'Goddamnit,' Parry muttered under his breath as he recognized the horse, still ground hitched. He wasn't bothered in the slightest about the loss of another man; in fact he was angry that the two men he had sent had failed to stop the buckboard getting to Calvary.

His crew had different thoughts. Two of their men now killed, and one left for dead. Were they chasing a gunny? They all knew Cal and he was no shootist. They'd already heard of Clancy's death, they'd left Haystack back on the trail, more dead than alive, and now Wilmington – or what was left of him – lay dead in the dirt. Burning down the Evans' place had been bad enough, but now it looked as if they were being led into a gunfight. They were cowhands, not gunfighters.

'We better get this one buried, boss,' one of the men said.

'We ain't got time and I ain't got the inclination. We ride on!' Parry growled. 'You can take care of him on the way back,' he added. 'Now, let's ride!'

The red mist that had filled Latham Parry's eyes was beginning to fade away as his scheming brain began to function once more. Reaching a crest in the trail, he called a halt. From here, he could look down into the valley where Calvary nestled peacefully amid a fertile plain.

The sun had disappeared behind the western horizon, and although it would be a full moon, for now it was clouded out. Parry took out his old army field glasses and focused on the twinkling lights that shone on Main Street, Calvary.

Parry was no fool. He felt like riding into town, guns blazing, but caution reigned. Evans's brother and that scumbag Cal Morgan must have made it to town, and given that Morgan knew Haystack and the two line riders, surely they'd put two and two together. Come hell or high water, Parry vowed that Cal Morgan would be the first to die.

Something wasn't right down there, Parry thought as he scanned the town. It was quiet – too quiet. The only lights showing were the street ones. Every building was shrouded in darkness.

'They know we're comin',' Parry said to no one in particular.

'What's the plan, boss?' one of the men asked.

Parry was unsure as to the next step. He'd been hoping to have the element of surprise on his side, but now that possibility had evaporated. He thought for a few moments, then said, 'We split up. I'll ride in from the west, you four men from the east. But keep your eyes wide open. I figure they'll be in the surgery. Douse some o' them street lights as you pass.'

'What then?' another asked.

'Get them arrows ready, we'll smoke 'em out. Be careful, though. They might have men posted out on Main.'

'Hell, boss, that could mean a shootout!'

'So?'

'So, none of us is a shootist. We signed on as cowhands, not killers.'

'Bit late for that, now,' Parry said with a smile that didn't reach his eyes. 'You wanna ride out? Go ahead.'

'Hell, boss, I ain't no quitter,' the man said quickly. He knew that if he tried to leave, Parry would backshoot him for sure.

'You boys will be well rewarded when this is all over, we'll have the Bar-Q and the Bar-B,' Parry said and there was a wistful look in his eyes.

None of the men asked any more questions or made any comments, but they all thought 'Yeah, if we survive'.

Now that his most trusted right-hand man had gone, Parry had no yardstick for the motley crew he was saddled with. He knew that the man who had spoken out was telling the truth: they weren't shootists – but then, neither were the townsfolk of Calvary.

Doc Mayweather was becoming increasingly concerned about his old friend, Josh Winters. The note he had received from Maria had been pretty explicit: Josh's health was failing fast, and he knew he needed to get out there to see him as quickly as possible. He knew Maria well, and she was not the sort of woman who would panic. 'Mitch, I have to get out to the Bar-Q,' the doc said in a hushed voice.

Mitch didn't reply straightaway. He rubbed his chin, then said, 'Could be signing your own death warrant, Doc.'

'I know, but I reckon if Parry and his men are heading here, they'll use the main trail from the ranch. They think they have nothing to fear, whereas I can ride over-land, and in the dark they won't even get a glimpse of me.' Mayweather waited for Mitch's response.

Mitch was silent, thinking.

'Son, I was born and raised in Calvary, I know this ter-ritory like the back of my hand. I ain't a gunman, so my use here is minimal – 'cept doctorin' – and Agnes will be here for that. She's more than just my housekeeper.' Again Mayweather waited.

'You sure about this, Doc?' Mitch asked.

'I've known Josh Winters for nigh on forty years, and anything I can do to help him, then by heaven, I'll do it.'

Mitch could tell that Doc Mayweather had made his mind up and that argument was futile.

'You go careful, Doc. You got a gun?'

'Sure, I ain't stupid.' The doc smiled and grabbed his bag. 'My horse is out back. I'll leave town by one of the alleyways. I could make the trip blindfolded.' Again he gave a reassuring smile.

The two men shook hands and Doc Mayweather left by the back door. The doc had been right about Agnes. She knew what he would do even before he did. She had the doc's horse saddled and hitched to the back fence. She'd also checked the Winchester and made sure it was fully loaded.

'Agnes, what would I do without you?'

'You'd never find your breeches, that's for sure,' Agnes answered. She was trying hard not to show her concern. 'You take care out there, Doc,' was all she said.

'You can be sure of it. I'll be back before you know it,' the doc smiled and mounted up. With a last smile, he waved and set off for the Bar-Q.

Latham Parry looked at the men who sat idly in their saddles. He knew most of them by name, but had confided in none of them. They were just cowhands, necessary for the smooth running of the ranch. Some were smoking and chatting, others slaking their thirst with the tepid water in their canteens. His gaze rested on one man.

He was younger than the rest of the crew and Parry didn't recognize him at all. He watched as the man lifted out his rifle from the saddle scabbard and checked the load, then replaced it. He then took out his handgun and checked the load in that as well.

'You,' Parry called out. 'I don't reckon I seen you before.'

The man calmly walked his horse closer to Parry. 'Name's Moran, Silas Moran, but most folks call me Si.'

'How long you been at the Bar-Q?' Parry asked. There was something about this man – boy really – he looked no more than eighteen or nineteen.

'Includin' today?'

'Includin' today,' Parry said.

'Three days, boss. Man called Clancy hired me.'

'Didn't say nothin' to me about any hirin',' Parry said.

The boy just shrugged.

Parry studied the boy. His clean, shaved face didn't look as if he could even grow a beard and his dark blue eyes looked at Parry unblinking. His build was slight, but his jaw was set firm, his face expressionless.

'You ever been to Calvary?' Parry asked.

'Nope, I was riding through your east range, didn't know I was trespassin', when I was stopped by the man called Clancy.'

'What made him hire you?' Parry asked.

Again, Si just shrugged. 'Asked me if I was looking for work, and had I ever worked with cattle, then offered me a job.'

Parry's brain was working overtime. He formulated a new plan.

'Well, I got a job for you. No one knows you in Calvary so you'll make an ideal spy. I want to know exactly where Brad Evans's brother is, as well as that rat Cal Morgan. Reckon you can do that?'

'Sure, piece o' cake,' Si answered.

'And find out how many men, if any, he's got lined up.'

'You figure they're waitin' on us?'

'There ain't no movement down there that I could see. The town's too quiet.' Parry took out his pocket watch and flipped the lid open. 'It's a quarter after six, town's usually busy. There's no one on the street. So, yes, I figure they're waitin' on us.'

'OK. I'll be back as soon as I can,' Si said. Without another word he wheeled his mount round and rode off to Calvary.

*

Twenty minutes later Si reined in at the edge of town. He took out his makings and rolled a cigarette, and igniting the Lucifer with his thumb, he lit up and drew deeply. It took another five minutes for Si to finish the cigarette, and in that time he saw not a soul. He could see the buckboard, horseless, parked on the side of Main Street, and a light shone from the saloon on the opposite side of the street.

He tossed the butt to the ground and walked his horse slowly towards the saloon; as good a place as any to start, he thought. Eyes and ears alert for any sound or movement, Si dismounted and hitched his pony to the rail. He took off his Stetson and banged the dust from his clothes as best he could, replaced his hat, adjusted his gun belt, and mounted the three steps to the boardwalk. He paused on the boardwalk and looked down Main Street, first to the left, then to right.

Nothing. No sound, no movement. Nothing.

He looked over the batwings and into the saloon. Lights were burning, three or four oil lamps were hanging on hooks fixed to the wall, and in the centre of the low ceiling hung an overly ornate chandelier, its glass baubles sparkling in the light from a dozen or so candles.

The wooden tables and chairs were cheap and arranged haphazardly, as if no one really cared. Glasses were left on the tables, along with a few cheap ashtrays, all overflowing. There were several paintings on the walls, stained by tobacco smoke. A few landscapes, and several of painted ladies in various poses that were meant to excite the customers, but to Si they looked ridiculous.

There was a long wooden bar running down the right-hand side of the saloon and a brass footrest broken by four none-too-clean spittoons. The floor was carelessly covered with well-used sawdust and didn't look as if it had been cleaned in weeks.

There were no customers. There was no one behind the bar either, the place was totally empty. The town looked and felt like a ghost town.

Si pushed open the batwings and stepped inside. Underfoot, glass crunched and the floorboards creaked. His hand rested on the butt of his Colt – just in case.

He walked to the bar and peered over it. The trap door was open and a black hole gaped open, looking like a portal to hell. On the wall behind the bar were shelves holding glasses, and a couple of dozen bottles, mostly cheap rotgut. A stained mirror was the centrepiece and on it, in gold lettering, it said: The Palace Saloon.

Si walked behind the bar-top and grabbed a bottle and a shot glass, then walked to the rear of the saloon, pulled out a chair and sat, his back to the wall and facing the batwings. He poured himself a shot and downed it in one, then refilled the glass and waited.

Thomas O'Malley, proprietor, barman and general dogs-body of the Palace Saloon, stepped outside the surgery to get some fresh air, rested his Winchester against the wall and took out his makings. O'Malley was in his late fifties, portly, and rather fat. He was a large Irishman who'd come to America in his youth. After the untimely death of his parents he had left New York and travelled west, but never made it past Calvary. He started working in the

Palace as a swampy and glass collector, before becoming barman. The then owner, Walt Fisher, was in his seventies, and not well. On his deathbed, in front of witnesses, he left the Palace to Thomas, and for the past twenty-five years Thomas O'Malley had been a contented man. His one regret was that he had never married. Sighing inwardly, he took out a paper and opened his tobacco pouch. It was then he saw the horse hitched outside his saloon.

He forgot about making a cigarette, grabbed his rifle and went to get Mitch.

'Mitch, Mitch! There's a stranger in town.'

'OK, OK! Calm down. Where is he?' Mitch asked, keeping his voice low.

'There's a horse hitched outside my saloon.'

'How'd you know it's a stranger?' Mitch asked.

'Who else could it be?' Thomas said with a straight face.

Mitch almost laughed, but held it in check. 'I'll go over and see who it is.'

'Hang on, Mitch. I'll come with you,' Cal said. 'You're a stranger here too, so everyone'll be a stranger to you.'

Mitch did laugh this time.

Cal grabbed his crutch and both men, after checking their guns for the umpteenth time, left the surgery.

'You recognize the horse?' Mitch asked.

'It ain't a Bar-Q horse, that's for sure,' Cal replied. 'Never seen him before.'

'That don't mean he ain't from the Bar-Q,' Mitch replied.

They reached the saloon and Mitch held up a hand

and put a finger to his lips. Silently he moved to one of the windows and took a look inside.

'There's a fella in the far corner,' Mitch whispered. 'Take a looksee.'

Cal peered through the window at the stranger seated quite calmly with a bottle in front of him.

'Recognize him?'

'No,' Cal replied. 'At least, I never seen him out at the Bar-Q.'

'OK, let's go in. Keep your gun hand close,' Mitch said.

He pushed through the batwings and both men entered the saloon.

'Beginning to think this was a ghost town,' the stranger said. 'Grab a glass, be good to have some company.'

'Thank you kindly,' Mitch said, and grabbed two shot glasses.

'Name's Silas Moran,' he said passing the bottle.

'Mitch Evans, and this here's my pard, Cal Morgan.'

There was an almost imperceptible change in Si's expression, but Mitch saw it.

'Cal Morgan?' Si said.

'You heard the name before?' Mitch asked.

'No, just making sure I heard you right,' Si replied.

Mitch knew he was lying. 'You passing through, or looking for work?'

'Work. You know of any?'

'Not around here. There's trouble brewing. Guess you made a wrong call stopping here tonight.' Mitch eyed the younger man carefully, looking for any change, however small.

Si casually picked up his shot glass and drained the contents. 'Guess I'll be moving on, then. Lubbock far?'

'Four, maybe five hours' ride,' Cal answered.

'Anywhere I can get some grub?' Si asked.

'Not tonight,' Mitch answered. 'If'n I was you, I'd hit the trail.'

'That a threat?'

'No, that's advice,' Mitch said and drained his glass. 'Thanks for the drink. You can leave the money – and the bottle – on the bar-top.'

'Reckon I'll keep the bottle. Town sure ain't a friendly place,' Si said.

'Ain't a good night for "friendly",' Mitch replied and stood up, followed by Cal.

As Mitch started to walk towards the batwings, followed by Cal, he stopped and beckoned Cal ahead. He had a funny feeling running through his belly. He waited and as Cal passed him, whispered, 'Get ready!'

Cal looked puzzled, but said nothing. Then Mitch heard the sounds he had expected, the scraping of a chair on the rough wooden floorboards and the metallic click of a hammer being pulled back. What followed seemed to be acted out in slow motion. In one fluid movement, Mitch pushed Cal to the floor and drew his Colt.

Two shots rang out almost simultaneously. One thudded harmlessly into the wall – the other found its target.

CHAPTER TEN

Doc Mayweather made good time getting out to the Bar-Q. He reined in on a low rise and looked down into the compound surrounding the house, barns and corral. It was eerily quiet, and the only light that shone came from the ranch house. Slowly he walked his horse down the slope and on to the main trail and headed towards the house. When he was fifty yards from the front porch steps he stopped, dismounted and grabbed his black bag. Leading his horse to the water trough, he headed for the house, his ears ringing in the silence.

As he mounted the porch steps a voice from inside rang out: 'Who's there?'

'Maria? It's me, Doc Mayweather. I got your note.'

The sound of the key turning in the large lock and the sliding back of bolts sounded unnaturally loud in the still of the night. Eventually the door swung open, revealing Maria with a worried and exhausted look on her face.

'Thank God,' Maria said and ushered the doc inside. She quickly relocked and bolted the front door.

'Perhaps I should see Josh first, I have many questions

to ask,' Mayweather said.

'Yes, yes, of course.' Maria led the way up to Josh's bedroom.

The room was in darkness and the air carried the scent of death. Mayweather opened the curtains and Maria lit a lantern.

Josh Winters' breathing was shallow and laboured. Mayweather felt for a pulse, then gave a deep sigh.

'The end is near, Maria,' he said in a strained voice. 'There's little I can do for him.'

Maria nodded. She knew in her heart of hearts that Josh was dying.

'What will you do when . . .?' Mayweather asked.

'I'll stay here,' Maria answered with iron determination in her voice.

'But won't the ranch have to be sold? I mean, Josh has no relatives.'

'He's left the ranch to me. The papers are with a lawyer in Lubbock.'

'Amos?' Mayweather asked.

'Yes.'

'Well, I'll be . . .' Mayweather said. 'You're gonna need all the help you can get to run this place and control Latham Parry.'

'Mr Parry will not be working here for much longer,' Maria stated.

'With luck, you might not see him again after today,' Mayweather said.

'Do you know what's going on?' Maria asked.

Doc Mayweather shook his head. 'Not all of it.' He went on to tell Maria the little he knew. Maria's face went from shock to horror.

'None of this was done with Josh's knowledge!' Maria said firmly.

'No one thinks it was. Brad Evans's brother is in town, along with Cal Morgan and some of the townsfolk. They're expecting Parry and his men at any moment, if he hasn't already arrived.' Doc Mayweather took out his pocket watch and checked the time.

Before they could continue their conversation, they both looked towards the large bed: Josh, his eyes wide open, was trying to say something.

Maria rushed to his side and leant down close to him. But Josh beckoned his old friend close, too.

His voice was weak, and punctuated with gasps of breath as he tried to delay death for as long as possible. 'Look – after – Maria. See – Amos.'

He broke off as a coughing fit took over.

'Don't try to speak,' Maria said. 'Rest, my love.'

Josh's eyes sparkled briefly as he heard her words – especially the last two. His face broke into a creased smile, he squeezed her hand once, then his grip went limp and his eyes closed.

Josh Winters died with the image of Maria's face the last thing he saw.

Mitch Evans and Si Moran stood facing each other, their handguns still smoking, and the smell of black powder wafted through the Palace saloon. A stony silence, made deafening by the explosions of the two Colts seconds earlier, filled the saloon. Cal, still lying on the floor, stared open mouthed, wondering why no more shots had been fired. Then it became obvious.

The barrel of Si Moran's pistol drooped downwards, then fell to the floor, and Moran's head sagged as he looked at the rapidly spreading blood that gushed from his chest. Then his legs buckled and he collapsed, face down on the sawdust-covered floor. The expression on his face was one of surprise more than pain, and as he fell, his eyes never left the face of Mitch Evans as if he expected him to fall dead as well.

'Goddamn!' Cal managed to utter. 'You knew he was gonna do that?'

'Kinda,' Mitch replied, and holstered his gun. 'You OK?'

'Yeah, I'm fine, thanks to you,' Cal replied. 'You reckon he's one of Parry's men?'

'He was. Something about him I jus' didn't take a likin' to. Let's get back to the doc's place. Parry won't wait much longer.'

'You hear that boss?'

' 'Course I heard it, I ain't deaf,' Parry almost spat out. 'Seems that kid, what was his name?'

'Si, boss, Si Moran.'

'Seems he reckoned on his gunplay. Couldn't tell if'n it was one shot or two,' Parry said, mainly to himself.

'What do we do now, boss?' another of his men asked.

'We ride, boys. We ride in and burn the hell outa that surgery and everyone in it!' Parry's voice began to rise, and there was a glint of madness in his eyes as he spoke that didn't go unnoticed by his men. But he didn't notice the looks that passed between his gang, so engrossed was

99

he in his hatred of Morgan, who, as far as he was concerned, had betrayed him. None of this would have happened if Morgan had done his job. Now he had Brad Evans's brother to contend with as well.

'Boss.' A tall, rangy man known as Cutter – no one knew his real name, and he never let on – spoke for the first time. 'Seems to me we got ourselves a situation here.'

'No shit,' Parry growled.

Cutter was not put off. Of all the men on the Bar-Q, he was not afraid of Parry. He was an ex-army sergeant with a mean streak. He always carried two Bowie knives, one in a sheath attached to the rear of his belt, the other inside his left boot. Cutter was a loner, and kept pretty much to himself – he did his job and no more.

'Sure, we can ride hell for leather into Calvary and maybe we can shoot up the town, burn the surgery down – and maybe the whole town. On the other hand, we know they're waiting for us. We got no surprise element left. We can ride into Calvary and sure as I'm sitting here we'll get cut down like dogs.

'So you want the Bar-Q? Well, it's just sitting there with an old man and a woman, maybe cookie and a couple of the older hands. They gonna put up a fight? Makes sense to me, we ride back to the ranch and wait for them to attack us and we do the cutting down.'

Cutter rolled himself a cigarette, lit it and drew deeply. Parry sat staring at Cutter, his brain working overtime. The rest of the men sat on their horses, furtively glancing at each other and desperately trying not to catch Parry's eye.

Parry didn't want to back down on his own plan, but

what Cutter said made sense: he'd have control of the Bar-Q, and they'd have the advantage over Morgan and Evans.

Suddenly he smiled, or at least as close to a smile as he ever got. 'I like it,' was all he said.

There was a palpable sigh of relief from the men. At least they wouldn't die today.

'Where the hell are they?' Thomas O'Malley was sweating heavily and the tension was getting to him. His question was answered by a knock on the front door.

'Who's there?' O'Malley shouted.

'It's me and Mitch,' Cal answered. 'Open up!'

O'Malley released the bolts and unlocked the door. 'What was the shooting about?' O'Malley asked. 'You two OK?'

'Yeah, we're fine,' Cal said. 'Seems Parry sent a new-comer into town and he figured on making a name for hisself.' Cal smiled. 'Mitch here shot him down, saved my bacon, too.'

Mitch, who had not uttered a word since returning, took off his hat and helped himself to a coffee.

'You been mighty quiet, Mitch,' Cal said, also grabbing a coffee.

'Thinking, is all,' Mitch answered absently.

'Wanna share those thoughts?' Cal asked.

'I was thinking, if Parry and his men were on the out-skirts of town, he would have heard those shots,' Mitch said.

'So?'

'So, if it was me, I'd know for sure that I was riding into

an ambush.' Mitch sipped his coffee and waited for any comments. When none were forthcoming, Mitch said to O'Malley, 'How often do you hear gunfire in Calvary?'

'Hell, the last time was over two, maybe three months ago, and that was a drunk who fell over and shot his own foot,' O'Malley said laughing.

'My point exactly,' Mitch said. 'What's the most vulnerable place right now? Here in town, or the Bar-Q?'

'Hell, you reckon they're gonna make a move on ol' Josh?' Cal said.

'That's what I would do. You read that note from Maria. Also the trail drive set off two days ago, so as far as we know there's only her, Doc Mayweather, and maybe one or two hands out there.'

Mitch watched the face of the men in the room before adding: 'I don't think they're coming into town.'

'We have to leave here, Maria,' Doc Mayweather said.

'Why? The house is secure. Josh made sure of that,' Maria said.

'No house is totally secure. We need to get Josh out and you off to Lubbock. If Parry gets back here with his men it'll be for a showdown. He won't know about Josh.'

Maria nodded slowly.

'Make sure you get the Will, and keep it safe. I'm sure Amos will have a copy, too. Then we can make it legal and above board, and tomorrow we'll arrange for Josh's funeral.' The doc wiped his brow and checked his watch again.

'I'll get a buggy sorted,' the doc began.

'No. I'll do it, I know where things are. But first let's

get Josh downstairs.' Maria went to the bed and drew the single sheet over Josh's body. 'Can we manage to lift him, do you think?' she asked.

'Of course,' Mayweather answered, and between them they managed to get the body down into the hall.

'There's some cord in the kitchen,' Maria said. 'If you can secure the . . . the . . . sheet, I'll hitch up the buggy.' With that she unlocked the front door and made her way to the barn.

By the time Maria had hitched up the pony and driven it to the house, Doc Mayweather had trussed up the body of Josh Winters and dragged it out on to the porch, and between them they loaded the corpse on to the buggy.

'Shouldn't take us more than three hours to get to Lubbock,' Mayweather said, as he hauled himself up into the driver's seat.

Maria had a sudden thought. 'Do you think we should leave a note?'

'Definitely not! Hell, 'scuse my language, Maria. If it comes to a gunfight in town and Parry wins, it'll be him that finds any note and he'll come after you.'

'But . . . I guess you are right,' Maria answered.

'Let's get to Lubbock, at least the night will be to our advantage.' With that, Mayweather released the brake, flicked the long-handled whip and they set off.

Having finished washing the few dishes from the evening meal, Beefsteak was making his way back to the cook-house, looking forward to a slug of whiskey from his secret stash. Then he saw Maria drive the buggy out of the barn, and watched transfixed as Doc Mayweather dragged what looked like a body from the front door of the ranch house. All thoughts of whiskey disappeared as he stared open mouthed at the scene. He stood stock still, undecided what to do.

Was Josh dead?

By the time he came to his senses, Maria and Mayweather had loaded the body on to the buggy and set off, heading north. Beefsteak dropped the dishes and shouted out, but they obviously didn't hear him. 'What the hell?' he mouthed. He ran to the bunkhouse – there were only four hands on the ranch, the rest were on the drive, except for . . .

He burst through the bunkhouse door, causing the four men inside, idly playing cards, to jump up in surprise.

'Something's goin' on down here, an' I don't like it,' Beefsteak yelled.

'What the hell you on about?' one of the hands asked.

It took Parry and his men forty minutes to get back to the Bar-Q. He called a halt on the rise that led down to the ranch house and outbuildings. It was pitch black and they were a good half-mile from the ranch house, but Parry was in no rush. He had waited years for this moment, so a few more hours wouldn't make any difference.

'OK, we split up. I want three men to the rear of the ranch house, the rest with me at the front. We'll go on foot from here. There might be one or two hands around, they'll need to be taken care of.'

'Even the cook?' one man asked.

' 'Specially the cook,' Parry said. 'He's been here years and worships the ground old man Winters walks on. Now make sure the back is covered, I don't want anyone to leave that house. Got it?'

The men nodded.

'Check your weapons and be alert,' Parry added as the men made their way in the dark towards the rear of the ranch house.

CHAPTER ELEVEN

'We gotta get out to the Bar-Q,' Mitch said. 'The drive has already started, so Maria, Josh an' the doc will be the only people there. If Parry gets there now he'll kill them all and take over the ranch. Someone tell the men outside, we gotta get to the Bar-Q. All those willing to ride, saddle up and let's get movin'!'

'Beefsteak'll be there, and at least four other old-timers,' one of the men said, 'they may be able to hold 'em for a while. I hear the ranch house is like a fortress.'

'Well, let's hope so,' Mitch said.

At that moment the front door swung open and Ellie-Rae stood in the doorway with a huge tray of coffee and a whole mess of beans and bread.

'Thought you fellas might be a tad hungry,' she said.

Mitch stood stock still, his mouth wide open – again.

'Cat got your tongue, Mr Evans?' Ellie-Rae said, a waspish smile parted her lips.

'Sorry, ma'am, er, Miss O'Hara, um, Ellie. Thank you so much, we'll have to eat on the trail though, we're heading out to the Bar-Q – now.'

'You take care out there, and get back here safely,' she

smiled at all the assembled men, but lingered longer when she looked Mitch in the eyes.

Clumsily, Mitch stepped forwards and took the tray from her hands – his own hands touched hers momentarily, and he felt like a thunderbolt had hit him. He almost dropped the tray.

'Careful there, Mitch, nothing worse than beans an' dust.' She smiled again and walked back to her small café.

'OK, lover boy, let's get movin',' Cal said.

'Put this in the back of the buggy,' Mitch said, ignoring the sniggers of the assembled company.

'Someone give me a hand here with the tray, then we need to hitch up the horses again,' Cal said.

Still grinning from ear to ear, Cal and several of the others followed Mitch to the livery.

'I suggest we go the back route, Parry won't know about that. I figure that's the way the doc went, too,' Al Chambers, the storekeeper said.

'We'll follow you, then – is it safe for the buggy?' Mitch asked.

'That's the only drawback,' Al replied. 'The buggy will have to use the trail.'

'OK, six men to ride with the buggy, the rest of you grab some bread and beans and let's go,' Mitch said. The men grabbed what food they could carry and left the surgery, filling their canteens as they left through the back door.

Mitch wasn't sure how many men Parry had in his gang, but he was certain that at least some of them were gunmen, and as far as he knew, he was the only gunman on this side of the fence.

He counted twenty men, including himself, and the six

men with the buggy. He wasn't sure how many of them had even fired a gun, let alone at someone. Still, he had to work with what he'd got. He dug in his spurs and followed Al, who was heading for the back trail to the Bar-Q.

Beefsteak was all but hopping from foot to foot as he tried to convey the urgency of his message.

'Jus' shut up an' listen,' he yelled, louder than anyone had ever heard him shout before. 'I jus' seen Miss Maria, Josh and Doc Mayweather leaving the ranch on a buggy. That can only mean two things. One, there's now only us here, and two, they must be expectin' trouble, and I think we all know who the trouble is likely to be!'

The four men threw their cards on the table and grabbed their Stetsons and weapons, making sure they had plenty of ammunition.

'We better head for the ranch house,' Beefsteak said. 'It's like a fortress over there. At least we can hold off Parry and his gunnies until help arrives.'

'What makes you think help will arrive?' asked one of the men as they ran across the compound towards the ranch house.

'Cos they wouldn't jus' leave us here without gettin' help,' Beefsteak replied, breathlessly.

They reached the ranch house and ran up the steps to the veranda, and then in through the front door. Beefsteak, the only one of the men to have been inside the ranch house before, hastily closed and locked the door, sliding the three sets of iron bolts across, and breathed a sigh of relief.

'Better check the back doors,' he said, and hurried

through to the kitchen, followed by the four rannies, their weapons drawn – just in case.

'It's OK,' Beefsteak said, 'they're both locked good and tight.'

They all removed their hats and sat at the kitchen table.

'What do we do now?' one of the men asked.

'We wait,' was all Beefsteak said.

Cal had urged the six outriders to go on ahead as the wagon was slowing everyone down and he knew that Mitch would need all the help he could get.

'The wagon's slowing us down too much,' Cal called out. 'You fellas ride on ahead, just make sure you don't run into Parry and his cohorts.'

'We can't leave you without support?' one man said.

'I'll be fine, I'm too far behind to run into Parry, now git goin' – Mitch is gonna need some back-up. I'll get there as soon as I can, now go!'

Reluctantly, the six riders urged their horses forward at first at a trot, then into a gallop.

Cal smiled. He knew Mitch would be as mad as all hell with him, but he knew it was a better plan. He knew the men were willing, but they were no gunnies, and as there was sure to be a showdown, he wondered how many of them had the courage to see it through to the end.

Cal concentrated on driving the buggy – by his reckoning he was around twenty minutes away from the Bar-Q, so he figured the six riders were maybe less than five minutes away. Cal hope they didn't go barging in gung-ho style. He should have given them instructions about what to do when they neared the ranch house, but. . . .

He urged the horses on, but they were already tired and no amount of whip-cracking would make them go any faster.

Patience. I need to be patient, Cal thought. Don't get het up, you'll get there when you get there.

Ellie-Rae was keeping herself busy in the café. There was nothing to do, as there were no customers. The town was deserted – even the mothers who had a daily cup of coffee and one of her home-made cakes while they waited for their children to finish school were missing as there was no school today.

She hoped there would be school tomorrow – not for business reasons, but because if there wasn't, it meant that Latham Parry had won.

And even more worrying, she might never see Mitch Evans again.

Parry and his men were struggling. Tethering the horses so far away had seemed like a good idea, as they could arrive quietly and not arouse the men Parry knew were in the bunkhouse, but walking in riding boots was no easy matter, even on a boarded sidewalk. Out here, in scrub, it was painful on both feet and backs, and they were only halfway towards the ranch house. If it weren't for the small cactus plants and sharp grass stalks, for two cents he'd take his boots off and walk barefoot.

Parry hoped the men he'd sent ahead to guard the rear of the ranch house were faring better than he was, but he doubted it. But he'd come too far to give up now. Tonight he hoped he would be the sole owner of the Bar-Q.

CHAPTER TWELVE

Doc Mayweather was getting tired. He knew that a man of his age should be at home, tucked up in a nice, warm, comfy bed, not driving a buggy with the body of his oldest friend in the back, and the woman who'd loved him all these years sitting beside him. They hadn't spoken a word for the last hour. There was nothing to say. It was Maria who broke the silence.

'Where will we stay in Lubbock?' she asked.

'An old friend of mine: Doctor Aloishus Wainwright Esquire,' Mayweather smiled as he said his friend's name. 'I think he's retired now. Just helps out the new doctor when he's asked.'

'You think he'll help us?' Maria asked.

'He'll fall over backwards to help, especially when he sees you,' the doc replied. 'He likes to think himself a Lothario.'

'Lothario?'

'A man who is a sexual predator – but although Aloishus loves all women, I don't think he's ever had one! Besides, he's well past it now. But for all that he's a kind

111

and generous man.'

'Is he married?' Maria asked.

'No, and never has been. He's given his life to healing folk. Never had the time for marriage.'

'That's a shame,' Maria said.

'You never married Josh. Now that is sad,' Mayweather said. As soon as he'd said it, he regretted it. 'Sorry, that was none of my business. I apologize.'

'There's no need. We should have married, but Josh didn't want me to marry a "cripple", as he put it. He wanted me to marry someone of my own age. But I loved him. And if he wouldn't marry me, I decided I wouldn't marry at all.'

'Josh was a very lucky man to have a woman like you,' Mayweather said.

They rode on in silence for a while until Mayweather pointed ahead.

'Lights! There's the lights of Lubbock,' he said delightedly, glad they had made it.

Thirty minutes later, Mayweather pulled up the buggy outside a detached, white-boarded, two-storey house complete with a white picket fence.

'What a beautiful house,' Maria said.

'Used to be the surgery, too,' Doc Mayweather said.

The front door flew open, and a very irate old man with a walking stick yelled out, 'What the hell you parkin' that heap o' junk outside my house for?'

Mayweather climbed down gingerly from the flat-back buggy.

'Seems you're as ornery as ever, Aloishus,' he said.

'Well, I'll be a. . . !' Aloishus exclaimed. 'That you, Doc?'

'Sure is! How are you, you ol' coot?'

'Lookin' better'n you by the looks o' things. Come on in – and who is that beauty you have the honour of accompanying?'

'I gotta unload the body of a dear friend and get the horses and wagon off the street in case. . . .'

'Tell me about it later. So let's get the body inside, then you can park the buggy round the back of the house – it's dark there, so no one will see it. Then take the horses to the livery over yonder.'

Between them, they carried the body of Josh Winters into the front room of Aloishus' house. There was a metal table still there from the days he practised, and carefully, they laid the body on it.

'I'll get some food and drink organized while you sort out the buggy and the horses.'

'Aloishus, this here is Maria,' Doc said.

'Right proud I am to meet such a beautiful woman,' Aloishus said, taking hold of Maria's hand and kissing it gently.

'See what I mean?' the doc said as he left the house.

'What was that all about?' Aloishus said.

'Oh, it was nothing, really,' Maria said, smiling.

'Come through to the parlour, I'll get us a drink,' Aloishus said. 'Tea or coffee?' he asked.

'Whiskey, neat, please,' Maria said.

'A woman after my own heart,' Aloishus said, opening up a cupboard set in the corner of the room.

'Good gracious, I've not seen such a selection of alcohol outside of a saloon!' Maria exclaimed.

'One tries to cater for all tastes,' said Aloishus, and

113

smiled as he picked out a bottle of genuine Scotch and two crystal tumblers.

'I think you'll find the Chivas Regal particularly smooth – it's 80 per cent proof and a blended whisky. This particular bottle is eighteen years old. I'm still waiting for the twenty-five-year old to arrive.'

Aloishus poured two generous measures and handed one to Maria. She swirled the glass and watched as the amber liquid swished against the crystal tumbler, then put it to her nose and sniffed it.

'It has a delicate bouquet, to use the wine parlance.' She then took a sip. 'Superb,' she said, 'as smooth as silk.'

'I'm glad you like it,' Aloishus said, taking a sip himself. 'Pure nectar,' he said, closing his eyes and savouring the mouthful. Aloishus' reverie was interrupted by the return of Doc Mayweather.

'Wagon's round the back and the horses are in the livery. Now we can relax. I'll call Amos in the morning and we'll meet later in the day. That OK with you, Maria?'

'Yes, that's fine,' she answered.

The doc noticed the Chivas Regal on the table. 'Broken out the good stuff, I see.' He went to the drinks cabinet and got himself a glass, and poured himself a very generous measure. Then much to Aloishus' chagrin, he knocked back the glass in one go.

'Ah, that's better,' the doc said.

'I'm surprised you even tasted it,' Aloishus said. 'Fifty-five dollars a bottle and you drink it like rotgut!'

The closer Latham Parry got to the ranch house, the more certain he became that Josh and Maria were no longer at home. There were lights showing in the down-stairs parlour and another in one of the upstairs bedrooms – Parry thought it was probably Josh's room. But there was no sign of movement anywhere in the house.

'Right,' Parry said to his men, 'keep guard on the house and the bunkhouse. If anyone, and I mean anyone appears, shoot to kill. Got that?'

'Yes, boss.'

'One of you get round the back of the house and tell the men there the same thing.'

'Where will you be, boss?' one of the men asked.

'Go get my horse, and make sure the canteen's full. I'm heading for Lubbock, I reckon that's where Maria and Josh have gone. But just in case I'm wrong, get ready for action. The Bar-Q is now under new ownership,' Parry said, smiling

CHAPTER THIRTEEN

Beefsteak and his crew were hiding behind the bunkhouse then, at his command, they made for the rear of the ranch house. The cook had left one of the back doors unlocked, just in case . . . and she let them in, quickly locking the door again. The men were all heavily armed, but greatly outnumbered, so they waited to see what Parry's next move would be. The cook and the other aged rannies saw Parry mount his horse and ride off on the north-westerly trail.

'Doggone it!' Beefsteak exclaimed. 'He's heading to Lubbock, an' that's where I believe the doc was taking Maria and Josh.'

'Well, there ain't nothin' we can do about that. The house is surrounded,' one of the men said.

'Yeah, but they can't get in,' Beefsteak told them. 'What if we get round the back of the house? There's only three men there, we can sneak up on 'em, take 'em by surprise 'cos they won't be expectin' anyone, will they?' Beefsteak was excited by his plan.

'We'll have to use knives, though. We don't want the

116

rest of the gang coming after us,' said Bart Wardle, the oldest man on the ranch. He might have been eighty or ninety, no one knew, including Bart!

'OK,' Beefsteak said, 'let's split up, an' keep your heads down.'

They were about to set off when another member of the gang came running round to the back of the house. A few words were exchanged, then the runner headed back to the front of the house, where he stayed.

'What in hell was that all about?' Beefsteak said.

'Damn fool, how're we supposed to know that? Can you lip read in the dark?' Bart said, and spat into the dirt.

'No need for sarcasm, you ol' coot,' Beefsteak responded. 'Let's git movin'!'

The five men made their way slowly towards the rear of the ranch house. They had no idea where the members of the gang were, so Beefsteak suggested they climb up a bit higher to see if they could catch a silhouette. Because the rear of the house was painted white, he hoped any movement would be obvious.

Beefsteak's hunch paid off. There, no more than twenty feet in front of him, was the outline of a hat. Beefsteak was dying to pull the trigger of his early model Winchester, but silence was the order of the day – or in this case, night. Making sure his rifle was in a position where he'd be able to find it later, he slithered on his pot belly down the slope. It was hard going for an old man, but Beefsteak was a very determined old man.

With his right hand, he reached for the knife that was sheathed on his belt by his backside. It was a large Bowie, a knife he used for everything, including cutting meat for

117

the rannies' meals.

Beefsteak brought the knife down in the blink of an eye. It entered just below the man's left shoulder blade, and such was the force of the blow, it penetrated the man's heart. He died instantly and silently.

Beefsteak made his way across the incline until he reached Bart's side.

'I got one of 'em,' he whispered. 'Now there's only two to get.'

Bart put a finger to his lips, then got up on to both knees and threw his hunting knife. There was an audible groan as the knife found its target.

'Only one, now,' Bart grinned.

'Where's Hal?' Beefsteak asked.

'Yonder, to the left,' Bart replied, indicating with a nod, 'and he's got the other fella in his sights, by the looks of things.'

Their conversation was abruptly halted by the sound of hoofs.

'What in hell. . . ?' Beefsteak said.

CHAPTER FOURTEEN

Mitch Evans raised a hand to halt his small band of greenhorns. He dismounted, pulling his Winchester clear of its scabbard. He motioned for the rest of the men to dismount and grab their weapons before ground-hitching their animals. Mitch pointed ahead. Peering into the darkness they could just make out a group of horses, also ground-hitched; no gunmen were visible. Parry must be sure of himself, Mitch thought.

The group crept forwards until they reached the animals; unhitching them, they smacked their rumps and sent them scurrying away from the Bar-Q.

'Well, that's the easiest part of what we need to do,' Mitch said.

'At least they can't escape,' one of the men said – Mitch thought that back in Lubbock he ran the haberdashery.

'We'll do what they did,' Mitch said. 'Leave the horses here and go in on foot.'

Just as he was about to start off, he heard the rumble of the wagon. Cal had made good time, he thought. Now they were up to full strength.

As Cal reined in, all seven men jumped to the ground, easing their aching backs and legs. The trail hadn't exactly been a smooth ride.

'Good to see you, Cal,' Mitch said.

'And you,' Cal replied.

'We've released Parry's horses . . .'

'I know,' Cal said. 'Thought we were being attacked! They came hurtling down the trail, but when they saw us they hightailed it off into the scrub.'

'We've heard no gunfire, so I guess they're staking the place out, waiting for Maria to come out, 'cos they'll think there sure ain't much hope of them breaking in.' Mitch grabbed his canteen and took a mouthful before offering it to Cal.

'No thanks, we had plenty of water, you save it,' Cal said.

'But the way I figure it, the house is empty. I reckon Doc Mayweather and Maria got Josh out of the house and on to a buggy.'

'That would account for no shooting, I guess,' said Cal.

'Then there's Beefsteak. Where the hell is he? There's a light showing in the bunkhouse, but I can't see no sign of movement.'

'How in hell can you tell that from this distance?' Cal asked.

Mitch reached into his jacket pocket and brought out a brass tube. 'Courtesy of the US Army,' he said with a grin.

'Mind if I take a look?' Cal said.

Mitch handed the telescope over to Cal.

'Nope. Can't see any movement. They're either dead or. . . .'

'. . . or in the house,' Mitch finished the sentence. 'And even Beefsteak couldn't get in that ranch house, unless. . . .'

'Unless what?' Cal asked.

'He's round the back of the house,' Mitch said.

'Well, there's only one way to find out.'

Mitch turned to the men. 'Cal and I are going to get round to the back of the house, and I want you men to fan out and slowly approach the house from the front. Parry and his men are almost certainly hidden on the slope there, waiting for Maria to make a move. So make sure your weapons are loaded and keep as quiet as you can – and one more thing: if you see movement, shoot to kill!'

CHAPTER FIFTEEN

Latham Parry slowly rode down Main Street. He didn't attract much attention – it was four in the morning, and the sun was rising in the east; already he could feel the warmth on his face.

He'd never been to Lubbock, so it was a question of riding slowly and looking for anything that indicated the presence of Doc Mayweather, Maria or Josh. He pulled his horse to a hitching rail, conveniently outside a saloon. A beer would go down well, and it would give him time to work out a plan. He got his beer and went to a table in the far corner of the saloon. He could see the whole saloon, including the batwings, so he could observe who came in and who went out.

He sat for an hour, nursing his beer and thinking. Then it was as if a flash of light came into his head. To move Josh they'd need a buggy, and if they had a buggy, they'd have horses. He downed what was left of his beer and went to hunt down a livery stable.

Mitch and Cal heard a whooshing sound, quickly followed by a grunt.

'Beefsteak?' Mitch said as loud as he could without shouting.

'Am I glad to see you!' Beefsteak said. 'We saw Parry head off to Lubbock, which is where Doc Mayweather took Maria and Josh.'

'We better get up there,' Mitch said to Cal, then turned to Beefsteak. 'The rest of the men are round the front of the house and behind Parry's men, so keep your heads down, OK?'

'You might let the men know we're here. Don't wanna be shot by my own side, that's for sure,' Beefsteak said.

'Don't you worry none, I'll tell 'em you're here, just keep down,' Mitch said.

From the front of the house gunfire opened up, pistol and rifle. 'Come on Cal, we better get to the horses and make our way to Lubbock, pronto.'

Both men ran, crouched as low as they could and made their way to where they'd ground-hitched the animals. They found Al Chambers guarding the animals and told him about Beefsteak and his four compadres at the rear of the house.

'OK, I'll pass the word along. Where're you two off to?' Al Chambers asked.

'Lubbock,' Mitch said. 'Beefsteak told us that's where the doc, Maria and Winters had probably headed. Seems Parry figured that out and he's on his way there,' Mitch told Al, mounting up as he spoke. Then he said, 'How long will it take to get there, Cal?'

'Should be there in an hour and a half at the outside. That's if these horses have the stamina.'

'Well, they've been fed and watered an' they've rested this past half hour, so they should be OK,' Al said.

'Let's vamoose,' Mitch said. 'Catch you later, Al, an' good luck.'

Latham Parry tied his horse to a hitching rail and walked back along Main Street. He figured that on foot he wouldn't stick out like a sore thumb. Within minutes, he found the livery. It was much bigger than he'd expected, with some forty odd stalls; a blacksmith was busy on his anvil, hammering out horseshoes.

'Help you, mister?' the smithy asked.

'Jus' takin' a look,' Parry said. 'Need my horse groomed and fed an' an overnight stay.'

'Well, we got room here,' the smithy said.

'Had any horses in today?' Parry asked, as if he was just making conversation.

'Have 'em all the time,' the smithy answered.

'You had a coupla buggy horses in?'

'What's your interest, mister?' the smithy was a tad concerned.

'Friends of mine said they might be in Lubbock. An old friend, Doc Mayweather, an' his friend, a Mex named Maria.'

The smithy visibly relaxed. 'Yeah, had a coupl'a nags in this afternoon. No Mex though, but a man said he was a doc. There was no buggy, though.'

'Thank you, friend, I'll be back in a short while,' Parry said and turned to leave, tipping his Stetson as he did so.

So where was the buggy? Perry tried to think what he would have done. In a barn? But he hadn't passed a building big enough to hide a buggy. The livery? Nope, the smithy would have said. It had to be near the livery, old man Mayweather wouldn't be able to handle two horses for very long.

Parry looked across the street. At this end of town there were mainly houses. He crossed the street and walked down an alleyway between two houses and looked from left to right. Then he saw it.

Exactly what I would have done, thought Parry. Hide it out in the open.

Parry smiled – an unusual event in itself – so this is where they are. Thought they were safe, did they? This time Parry laughed. He had plenty of time now, he'd take his horse to the livery and find a room for the night. Night would be the best time. He patted his knife and led his horse to the livery.

'Howdy again, mister,' the smithy said.

'Howdy, can I book my horse in for a feed, groom and an overnight stay?'

'Sure thing, mister. You want him washing as well as grooming?'

'Yeah, why not. Spoil the critter, he's had a tough day,' Parry said.

'That'll be two dollars, mister. You want me to check his shoes, too?'

'Yeah, do that. Can you recommend a decent bed and breakfast?'

'Sure, try Widow Hawkins, she does a steak that was made in heaven,' the smithy said, almost drooling at the thought.

'Thanks, here's two dollars, let me know if any of the

shoes need replacing, OK?'

'Sure thing, Mr . . .'

'Jenkins,' Parry said. 'Claude Jenkins.'

'Will call on you if the shoes need replacing, Mr Jenkins.'

Parry tipped his hat and turned to leave. He stopped.

'Where do I find Widow Hawkins?' Parry said.

'Cross the street, third house from the end,' the smithy replied.

'Many thanks,' Parry said, and lifting off his saddle-bags, he left the livery stables.

Mitch and Cal were making good time. The horses seemed fresh and willing, it was almost as if they were racing each other.

'How far now?' Mitch asked.

Cal was looking around the terrain, remembering the last time he went to Lubbock.

'Another half hour should do it. I ain't been to Lubbock for a while, but I'm beginning to recognize the trail. Over the next rise we should be able to see the town lights.'

'Let's hope we're not too late,' Mitch said.

'Lubbock's a big town, there's talk of it being the regional seat of Texas one day, who knows? Unless he's lucky, it'll take him a while to track them down.'

'I doubt it very much,' Mitch said. 'A buggy, an old man, a dead body and a Mexican woman? They ain't gonna find it easy to hide.'

'Unless Maria or the doc knows someone in Lubbock who'll not ask any questions,' Cal said.

126

'Must be the doc,' Mitch said. 'Maria hasn't left the ranch for years, so I was told.'

'Another doc?' Cal thought aloud.

'Could well be. But you know what? I'd start at the livery stables. They gotta rest the horses and hide the buggy. We find the horses, we find them.'

'Trouble is, if we can suss that, so can Parry!' Cal said.

Before Mitch could reply they reached the crest of the bluff, and ahead saw the twinkling lights of Lubbock. Mitch felt as if he could almost reach out and touch them.

'Come on,' he said, 'we're almost there!'

Al Chambers had had enough of waiting. He gathered a group of men around him and suggested a plan.

'We ain't doin' much good just sittin' on our butts,' Al started. 'I reckon we take on this gang and finish it. For all we know the doc, Maria and Josh could still be in the ranch house biding their time.'

'Ain't likely, is it?' one of the men voiced his opinion.

'Sure it's likely. That house is like a fort, in fact, more secure than any fort I ever did see,' Al said, getting a tad uppity.

'An' how many forts 'ave you seen?' another man asked.

'More than enough. I was in the US Cavalry for ten long years,' Al said, quite calmly.

'I never knew that,' the barber said in a voice that was too loud.

'Keep your voice down, you'll give our presence and position away, you damn fool,' Al looked daggers the man.

'Sorry, Al. Nerves, I guess. Known you goin' on for fifteen years an' never knew that, is all.'

Al resumed. 'I suggest we fan out and pick a target. At the moment they don't know we're here, so we got that element of surprise. Take careful aim when you have a target, and then keep your heads low, keeping an eye on your quarry. If your target returns fire you'll know two things: one, you ain't killed him, and two, you'll know his position from the muzzle flash. So try and finish the job. Got it?'

'Sure thing, Al,' the barber replied.

'OK, let's move. Quietly.'

The first shot rang out within minutes of the men dispersing. A strangled yell, more like a scream, echoed from below. A body rose to its knees and then fell forwards.

'I think that's a sure fire hit!' the barber said.

'Could be right there,' Al said, a grin on his face.

The shooting became more and more frenzied as fire was returned, but the men followed Al's advice and kept their heads low enough to avoid being shot, but high enough to see muzzle flashes. Having the higher ground certainly paid dividends – the men below had to stand in order to take aim at a target, but more often than not they were hit before they could fire a shot. Within minutes of the start of the shooting, there came a deadly silence.

'Have we got 'em all?' one of the townsfolk said in hushed tones.

'If we haven't, they sure have gone quiet. Maybe they hightailed it to get their horses.'

'Well, if they did they're in for a shock an' a long walk.'

The conversation came to a sudden halt as a light appeared in the hallway of the ranch house.

'Damn!' Al said. 'They musta been in there all the time.'

Slowly the great wooden door opened and the men got ready to shoot in case it was the gunnies who'd somehow got into the ranch house. But standing there, with a lamp held high so he could be seen, was Beefsteak.

'Damn!' Al said again, 'How in tarnation did he get in there?'

'Howdy, boys!' Beefsteak called out.

Al walked down the incline towards Beefsteak, a smile on his face now. Beefsteak walked towards Al and they started to shake hands, but Beefsteak broke off and gave Al a bear hug.

'Seems we got 'em,' Beefsteak said.

'We? Didn't see you shootin' much,' Al said.

'Goldarn it, who d'you think took care of those critters at the back of the house?' Beefsteak said, indignantly.

'Sorry, Beef. Just I didn't hear no shots comin' from there,' Al said.

'That's cos we used our knives so's not to give the game away,' Beefsteak grinned.

'How in tarnation did you get into the house?' Al asked.

'I got a key to the back door. The root cellar is right under the kitchen, so I comes in when the hands want feedin'.'

'Well, I'll be a son . . .'

'Where's Mitch and Cal?' asked Beefsteak.

'They rode out to Lubbock. Figured that's where Doc Mayweather, Maria and Josh went,' Al said. 'They asked who the doc knew in Lubbock and I tole them old Doc Wainwright was Merryweather's oldest friend an' if I was a betting man, that's where I'd put my money.'

'They sure did. I see'd them go, but I'm afeared ol' man Josh is dead,' Beefsteak said.

'Seems like Parry already headed that way,' Al said. 'Left his men here to take over the ranch and kill you and the hands in the bunkhouse. Parry knew you'd still be here.'

'We'd better get to Lubbock,' Beefsteak said.

'It'll be too late – one way or the other,' Al said, and grudgingly, Beefsteak agreed.

Mitch and Cal arrived in Lubbock, surprised the town was so quiet. What had Parry planned to do? Kill Josh and Maria?

It didn't take them long to find the house of Aloishus Wainwright; seems everyone knew the old doc. Dismounting at the rear of the building, they knocked on the back door.

'Who's there,' a voice from inside the house called out.

'It's Mitch and Cal. We came to help you folks. Parry should be here by now.'

Slowly the back door opened and Doc Wainwright, once he'd taken a good look at the two men, holstered his gun and unlocked the back door.

'Cal, you take the front of the house and I'll take the rear. Doc, you take Maria and Josh upstairs.'

'I'm afraid old Josh is dead,' the doc said.

'I sure am sorry to hear that,' Cal said.

'Me too,' Mitch added and removed his Stetson, nudging Cal to do the same.

'No time for mourning yet,' Doc Wainwright said. 'We better get organized.'

Swiftly, Cal moved to the front of the house and Mitch, dousing the oil lamp in the kitchen, stood and waited, his Colt on the kitchen table, his Winchester held tightly against his chest.

They didn't have to wait long.

'We got company,' Mitch said.

Cal was at the front of the house where he had a good view of Main Street: he had seen the lone figure, but hadn't been able to see his face clearly. As soon as he heard Mitch call, he went to the back of the house, his rifle loaded and ready to fire. Doc Mayweather and Maria slept soundly, but Aloishus Wainwright joined them in the kitchen.

'What's going on?' Wainwright asked.

'Sorry to wake you Doc, but seems we have a visitor,' Mitch said.

'You didn't wake me, who's the visitor?'

'Not sure yet, but I think it's Latham Parry,' Mitch said.

'Alone?' Wainwright asked.

' 'Pears to be,' Mitch said. 'But there could be others lurking nearby.'

'Well, let's find out if he's alone, and if he is, what he wants,' Aloishus said.

'We know what he wants,' Mitch said. 'He wants the Bar-Q, and to get it, he has to kill Josh and Maria.'

131

'I doubt he knows yet that Josh died a little while ago,' Cal added.

'He's already burned out the Bar-B, and killed my brother, his wife and child,' Mitch said.

'Brad, Julia and Jon?' Doc Wainwright sat down in shock.

'You knew them?'

'Knew them! I helped Doc Mayweather deliver Jon. So yes, I knew them. I'm so sorry for your loss.'

Wainwright leaned forward and put his head in his hands.

There was a knocking on the front door. Mitch and Cal instantly had their handguns out and left the kitchen. They walked down the hallway keeping close to the walls on each side until they reached the door. Standing each side of it, it was Mitch who called out: 'Who's there?'

'It's Ellie,' a voice answered.

Mitch turned the large key in the lock, released the bolts top and bottom and yanked open the door and pulled Ellie-Rae into the house before quickly closing and locking the door pushing the bolts back into position.

'How did you know we were here?' asked a puzzled Mitch.

'I didn't. I was heading for the Bar-Q and heard the shooting. It went on for some time and I was afraid that the outlaws would ride down the trail, straight towards me, but the only thing that thundered from the Bar-Q was a bunch of riderless horses. But on the trail past the turn-off for the Bar-Q I saw buggy tracks. I put two and two together and figured Maria and Josh, along with Doc

Mayweather, had left the ranch and were heading for Lubbock, so that's why I'm here. I knew Doc Mayweather was an old friend of Doc Wainwright and . . .'

Ellie-Rae paused, lowering her head, and Mitch was sure she was blushing.

'And what?' Cal asked, knowing full well what the reason was.

'I wanted to make sure that Maria was safe,' Ellie-Rae said. 'And of course Josh, too.'

Mitch stepped forward and held Ellie by the shoulders. 'I'm afraid Josh passed away back in his own bed at the Bar-Q. Natural causes,' he added.

Tears welled up in Ellie-Rae's eyes, and Mitch pulled her closer to him, their bodies touching. To be truthful, Mitch thought to himself, I'd have pulled her closer even if she hadn't start to cry. Their mutual embrace was cut short by a small cough from behind Mitch.

'Sorry to interrupt your, er, greetings, but we still got a prowler outside who's taking a mighty big interest in our ol' buggy.'

'Sorry Cal, this here's Ellie-Rae.'

'I know, I met her too. Remember?'

'Sure, 'course I do. Just wasn't sure if you'd remembered her.'

'Well, you sure did,' Cal gave him a wink and a wicked grin before joining Aloishus in the now darkened kitchen.

'He still out there, Doc?'

'Sure is, been clambering all over the wagon,' Aloishus said, staring into the dark night. 'I reckon he'll try breaking in when he thinks we've all gone to bed.'

133

'Reckon you could be right, Doc,' Cal said.

Mitch entered the kitchen, followed by Ellie-Rae. After the introductions, Aloishus suggested they take turns in guarding the house against what he called 'intruders'.

'You got a spare bedroom, Doc?' Mitch asked.

'Got three spare bedrooms, so there's a bed for everyone.'

Aloishus took Ellie-Rae's hand, and as he'd already done with Maria, raised it to his lips and kissed it.

'My lucky day,' he said. 'Two beautiful ladies under my roof.' He sighed, smiling. 'This way, ladies.'

Doc Mayweather had followed Mitch into the kitchen, and said: 'He sure doesn't change!' Then he said: 'Now, as I've already had a nap, I'll take first watch. I'll wake you in two hours, Mitch.'

'OK, goodnight Doc, I'll try and prise your friend off the women and find out where we sleep.'

'Goodnight boys, see you later,' Mayweather said as he picked up his rifle and settled on the chair by the window, scouring the outside.

Latham Parry was undecided as to his plan of action. He was a gunfighter, but there were at least four men in the house – certainly, two of them were old men, but they could still handle a weapon. He wished now that he'd brought a couple of men with him, but he'd had a rush of blood to his head. By now his men would be in the Bar-Q ranch house, only to find it empty, and he was stuck in Lubbock outnumbered and outgunned. He sat and thought, and an idea jumped into his head: fire.

He'd burn them out.

The buggy was close to the rear of the house and the wood was bone dry. He scouted around for twigs and brush, and he also found some tumble-weed. He piled the debris under the wagon and took out a box of lucifers. Striking one with his thumb, it took only seconds to produce a healthy blaze. The wagon caught fire and the flames soon leapt high, the heat scorching the rear of the house.

Inside the kitchen, Doc Mayweather had walked to the pot-bellied stove and refilled his mug with coffee. He could smell smoke, but assumed it was from the stove. He put his mug down on a counter while he settled himself back on his chair. As he reached for the coffee, he saw the flames. He dropped the mug and ran as fast as he could to the foot of the stairs.

'Fire, fire, FIRE!' he called out. There were rumblings from the rooms upstairs and Mitch and Cal were the first ones down. Quickly they knocked on the other doors warning that the house was on fire.

Maria was more concerned about Josh. 'We must get him outside,' cried. 'We can't leave him here!'

'Don't worry,' said Mitch, 'we'll get the living out first, then we'll carry Josh out, don't worry.'

Everyone was now downstairs, but Mitch stopped them from going outside: he knew what Parry was up to – if they went outside he'd pick them off one by one.

'Cal, we need to distract Parry,' said Mitch. 'Only thing I can think of is one of us goes out the back door, and the other, the front. I'll take the back.' For the first time, fear showed on the face of Ellie-Rae. Not for herself, but for Mitch Evans.

135

CHAPTER SIXTEEN

Al and Beefsteak had both been quiet for at least five minutes before Beefsteak suddenly broke the silence.

'I don't care if I am too late,' he said. 'I'm ridin' to Lubbock.'

'Well, there ain't no point you goin' alone,' Al said. 'I'm goin' with you.'

'Let's ask and see if any of the men wants to join us,' Beefsteak said.

'OK, but remember, none of us is a gunnie!'

So Beefsteak put it to the men, that they needed three or maybe four men to go with them – and added that the rest should stay in the house '. . . in case there's any o' them shootists out there.'

Within seconds every man's arm was raised in the air.

Beefsteak looked to Al. 'OK, you choose four.'

Al's solution was clear: 'All men who are married take one step back. Now, all the men with children, take a step back. Single men, take a step forwards.'

Then turning to Beefsteak he said, 'There's our four men.'

'OK,' Beefsteak said, 'fill your canteens and make sure we got a coffee pot and some jerky.'

'Beefsteak,' Al said, 'it's only an hour and a half to Lubbock from here.'

'Better safe than sorry,' was Beefsteak's instant reply. 'OK, let's get to the horses and mount up, men.' Al led the way, his legs defying his age.

Three of their horses were missing.

'You thinkin' what I'm thinkin'? Beefsteak said.

'Sadly, yes. Three of Parry's men have hightailed it to Lubbock. Damn!'

'Mount up men, we don't have much time,' Beefsteak yelled, almost frightening his horse.

The ride was hazardous, and it wouldn't be light for about two, maybe three hours, by which time they'd be in Lubbock.

Parry's men were doing much better. Although they didn't know it, they had almost an hour's start on the Bar-Q men. They knew they'd be followed as soon as it was discovered their horses were missing, but that didn't bother them. The prize of the Bar-Q and a share of the profits would keep them in relative luxury for the rest of their lives.

They could already see the lights of Lubbock ahead. There weren't that many at this time of the morning, but they knew they'd find Parry. They also knew Parry would find Maria and Josh. Once those two were out of the way, from then on it'd be easy living for him.

The lead rider reined in. 'Seems pretty quiet down there, I reckon we split into two groups, half to enter town from the east, the other from the west. Keep your eyes and ears open, and your guns at the ready.'

'What in hell's that?' One of the men pointed.

In the distance they could see flames and sparks leaping up into the air. 'I think we've found Parry,' the lead rider said, a grin on his face. 'Giddup!' and he dug his spurs into his mount's flanks and the gang galloped freely towards Lubbock.

CHAPTER SEVENTEEN

Mitch Evans ducked low and made his way to the back door to his left. He could feel the heat of the flames on his face. The right-hand door was burning fiercely, and if it wasn't doused soon the whole house would be engulfed in flames. Gently, and as quietly as he could, Mitch twisted the door handle and pulled the door towards him. The top hinge creaked, sounding to Mitch like a herd of stampeding buffalo. He stopped pulling and waited.

The only sounds he heard were the crackling of the flames and the footsteps of the others coming from the hallway. He pulled the door closer to him – it was almost wide enough for him to squeeze through. But still he waited.

No shots rang out, so he edged the door wide enough for him to crouch down and leave the house. He peered round the rear of the house. The wagon was a blazing wreck, and standing behind it was Latham Parry, his face red from the heat of the fire.

Mitch backed into the kitchen and made his way back to the hall, where everyone was waiting, wondering which way to go.

'Parry's out the back, use the front door and make for the livery stable. Cover Josh in straw in a separate stall, the rest of you spread out as best you can. I'll take care of Parry.'

'I'll stay with you,' Cal said.

'No! You take care of everyone. I can handle this, then we'll wake up the hotel and try and douse the fire – now git!'

Mitch rushed back to the kitchen, his Colt cocked and ready, half expecting to see Parry – but there was no sign of him in the house. Once again he stepped through the open door, and saw Parry still standing behind the burning wagon, staring upwards, watching the hot red embers rising into the moonless sky.

Surely someone would see them. But Lubbock was still asleep.

Mitch took aim. His hand was shaking, but he was determined. He pulled the trigger – and missed.

Parry didn't even move his position. He calmly took out his own side-iron and looked along the side of the house that wasn't burning, making sure he knew where the shot had come from.

Mitch decided not to use his Colt again. He grabbed a Winchester rifle that was on the kitchen table, made sure it was loaded – and was immediately knocked flat on his back, out cold, with a shot to the side of his head.

*

Cal heard the two shots, the first a rifle, the second a pistol. Then, silence. That immediately had Cal worried.

'What the hell is going on,' he said to no one in particular. 'Everybody stay put, I gotta make sure Mitch is OK.'

'Just be careful,' Maria said.

'I'm coming with you,' Ellie-Rae said.

'Not until I see what's happened over there. The flames are getting higher. Please, stay here in the livery, it's safer. If all's clear I'll call you over. But if you don't hear from me get ready to shoot. Got that?'

'OK,' Ellie-Rae gave way. 'But you better call me!'

'Right, I'm goin' out the side door, I'll double back behind the general store, then I'll cross the street and go down the alleyway. Just don't shoot me, OK?' he said with a grin.

'I'll think about it,' Ellie-Rae said, also with a grin.

'Make sure you get that Will to Amos and get it certified, Maria. Then you're home and dry – well, dry anyway,' Cal said, a smile on his face.

Cal left the livery, and Ellie-Rae saw him cross the street and disappear down an alleyway. But then she heard the sound of hoofs. She ducked behind the large wooden door and saw three riders. She recognized the horses – but not the riders.

'What'll we do? They must be Parry's men. Does that mean all our men are dead?' Ellie-Rae was frantic.

'Now calm yourself down, lassie,' said the doc. 'It doesn't mean a thing. Could be those three managed to escape.'

The three horsemen rode past the burning building

141

and entered the next alleyway along. Quickly they dismounted, and ran through to see a buggy like a giant bonfire. Of Parry, there was no sign.

'Hold it right there, mister!' a voice from the side door commanded.

'Parry? It's us. They damn well killed everyone else. We were lucky to get out alive.'

'How many men did they get?' Parry asked.

'Impossible to tell. They came from behind us, they held the high ground, we just couldn't see how many there were. Sorry, boss.'

'We better get mounted up, folks'll be out soon as they smell the smoke. We'll wait across the street in an alleyway, and anyone leaving this house we shoot. An' I mean shoot to kill. Got that?' Parry looked at each man in turn.

They mounted up and rode two blocks down, crossed Main Street, rode behind the buildings and doubled back until they were right opposite the now burning building. The flames at the rear of Aloishus's house had reached the shingles and were spreading rapidly – but still no one came out of the front door.

Cal reached Mitch's side and knelt down, feeling for a pulse. He saw the pool of blood that almost surrounded Mitch's head, but the pulse was strong – the bullet had grazed Mitch's head just above his left ear, and hadn't hit bone.

Mitch coughed, and opened one eye. 'You took your time,' he said, a wry grin on his face.

'You were this far from being a dead man,' Cal said, holding his thumb and index finger almost touching, 'but it's only a scratch.'

'Where's Parry?' Mitch asked.

'Three of his men showed up. They waited a while to see if anyone left the house, and I guess they figured you'd all left. They just rode off, back to the ranch I'd say.'

Mitch sat up; he felt a little dizzy but no pain, at least none that he couldn't handle.

'Give me a hand up, will ya?' Mitch said.

Cal grabbed his arms and pulled Mitch to his feet. The heat of the flames was by now almost burning his face and drying out his eyes.

'Let's get out of here and back to the Bar-Q. I got me a feeling we might be needed.'

The fire wagon turned up just as Cal and Mitch left the alleyway.

'You fellas OK?' the driver of the fire wagon asked as he noticed the blood that covered the left side of Mitch's face.

'Yeah. We're fine. The culprits just left town, we're gonna chase 'em down,' Cal said.

From the livery, Maria, Ellie-Rae and both docs crossed Main Street. Ellie-Rae immediately went to Mitch.

'You know these two?' asked the fire wagon driver.

'Sure do. We'd all be dead if it wasn't for them,' Aloishus said.

They parked the fire wagon at the side of the house and two men manned the pump, while two others took the huge hose towards the rear of the house.

'OK, start to pumping!' a voice shouted out.

The two men on the fire wagon began pumping furiously and water was shooting out the house at the base of the fire and slowly moving upwards.

A second wagon arrived at the scene. This one carried spare water tanks.

'Damn,' Parry said. 'They're gonna put that fire out!'

'Guess they vamoosed, boss,' one of the men said.

'You don't say,' Parry's sarcasm all too obvious. 'Let's head back to the Bar-Q and finish this matter. If they're headed that way, we might even catch 'em.'

The four men wheeled their animals round and rode down Main Street back towards the Bar-Q. No one took much notice of them – the fire was much more interesting.

Mitch and Cal watched the four horsemen as they left the alleyway. 'That's Parry. Looks like they're going to head back to the ranch,' Cal said.

'Then we better get goin',' Mitch said. 'I got a feeling we might be needed!'

Despite their age slowing them down, Al and Beefsteak and the four hands were making good progress. Already they could see the lights of Lubbock – and the flames.

'What in tarnation is that?' Al asked.

'Seems to me Parry has arrived,' Beefsteak said.

'Make sure your rifles are loaded, and rest them across your lap. You might need 'em pretty damn quick,' Al said.

'Reckon it's another half hour before we hit Lubbock,'

Beefsteak said.

'You reckon Parry will go back to the ranch?' Al asked.

'That's what I'd do,' Beefsteak replied, assuming they were too late and Parry had won this battle, but not the war.

They rode on in silence, scanning the horizon, looking for any movement.

CHAPTER EIGHTEEN

'We gotta get you back to the ranch,' Mitch stated. 'We don't want Parry to take the ranch by force. But first we'd better check the lie of the land at the back of the house.'

'We'll get ready,' Maria said.

'No!' Mitch almost shouted. 'Just me and Cal! I want the docs to look out for you. We have no idea how many of Parry's men are still there, or indeed, how many we have left, so I'm not putting you two ladies in any danger.'

'This is not your fight,' Maria said.

'It is now,' Mitch said, rubbing his head. 'Me an' Cal are gonna recce behind the house, see if we can catch any sign of Parry. We'll get the buggy ready and let the undertaker know where Josh is. Doc, you and Aloishus escort these two ladies back to the Bar-Q.'

'Maria,' Cal started, 'It's important that you and Ellie-Rae are safe and away from Parry's clutches. You know as well as I do that should he find you, he'll kill you to get the Bar-Q.'

Mitch walked over to Ellie-Rae and said: '. . . an' I sure don't want anything to happen to you.'

Mitch reached for her hand, but spontaneously she threw her arms around his neck and they kissed. Mitch knew how he felt about her, and holding her body against his, he now knew how she felt about him.

'We'll catch you up on the trail,' he whispered into her ear, 'I promise.'

She hugged him tightly, then backed away. 'You better had,' she said. 'You better had.'

As Al and Beefsteak and the four hands rode towards Lubbock, dawn was beginning to make itself felt. The black of night was turning into a murky grey, and every man knew that within minutes, the sun would make an appearance. But who this would benefit the most was open to question.

Beefsteak declared: 'I'm gonna ride up that slope yonder and use my telescope, see if I can see any movement ahead or behind us. Keep a lookout for me – I'll sign if we're being followed.' He didn't wait for a response, but just pulled his mount to one side and made his way up the slope. As he neared the top of the slope he stopped: he didn't want to make a silhouette of himself against the brightening sky. He took out his 'scope and scanned the trail. The land was flat for as far as the eye could see, and Beefsteak focused and refocused the 'scope as he swept along the trail.

Then he saw a dust cloud, though he couldn't make out the riders, or even how many there were. Then a mile or so further back he picked out another dust cloud.

'What the hell. . . .' Beefsteak couldn't distinguish friend from foe, and knew he'd have to wait until he could get a better view. The front group was almost within range for him to be able to recognize a face or a horse. Just a few more minutes, he thought to himself.

'Parry!' he said out loud. 'Latham Parry, by all that's holy. That sonuvva is still alive, goddammit!'

He turned to his own men and saw that Al was looking at him. Beefsteak waved and held up four fingers. Al nodded, showing Beefsteak he understood.

Beefsteak now concentrated on the second group. They were still too far away but again, pretty soon they would be in range. Beefsteak was not a patient man and sat on his saddle, his fingers tapping on the pommel and sighing and cursing at the same time. He looked through the scope. They were almost in range. He kept the 'scope to his eye and then realized he was looking at Mitch, and with him he could make out Cal.

Then suddenly there was the sound of a shot: the bullet caught his horse in the neck and silently the animal dropped its head and it crumpled to the ground.

'What the hell. . . .' was all Beefsteak could say, as his horse had trapped his right leg: with his foot still in the stirrup, his hip was bearing the whole weight of saddle and horse.

Al heard the gunshot and took out his 'scope, looking to where he'd last seen Beefsteak. He was nowhere in sight.

'Keep to the trail, I'm riding back to check on Beefsteak.' He wheeled his horse round and rode off the trail, intending to climb the slope from the other side.

Dismounting just before the summit, he tethered his horse and climbed the few feet to look over the crest. He saw Beefsteak straightaway, pinned under his dead horse. Al slid down to the old-timer's side, and placing his hands under Beefsteak's armpits, he pulled with all his might.

It took all Al's strength and the free leg of Beefsteak's to get him out from under his horse, and it looked as if his leg might be broken.

'How you feelin', Beef?' Al asked.

'Sore, but OK.'

'I'll help get you up and over to the other side, and we'll take a look at your leg,' Al said.

'It ain't broke,' Beefsteak said. 'Just bruised some.'

'We'll see,' Al said, not very convinced. 'We'd better get back to the Bar-Q, at least we stand a better chance of defending ourselves.'

'You hear that?' Cal said.

'Sure did, weren't that far away, either,' Mitch said.

'Wonder who was shootin'?' Cal said.

'Doubtless we'll soon find out,' Mitch said, then set his horse to a gallop.

Up ahead he could see a dust cloud and instinctively knew it was Parry. As the trail took a sweep to the left, he noticed another dust cloud. Reining in he took out his 'scope: he could see the wagon, and breathed a sigh of relief.

Then he noticed there were no riders. Where were Al and Beefsteak?

Mitch set off at a gallop again, and this time he left the

trail and headed for the bluff on the left-hand side of the trail. Cal followed – he didn't ask what was going on, he had heard the gunshot and could see the dust up ahead.

They reached the bluff and rode to the summit. Mitch and Cal dismounted, grabbing their rifles as they did so.

'Boy, am I glad to see you two,' said a relieved Al.

'You OK, Beefsteak?' Cal asked.

'Yeah. Just bruised my leg when the horse fell on me.'

'Looks broken to me,' Cal said.

'Well it ain't!' Beefsteak was adamant.

'OK. Let's get him down to the wagon,' Mitch said. 'Parry ain't that far behind.'

Cal and Mitch helped Beefsteak on to Mitch's horse, then Mitch mounted behind him and slowly they rode down the slope to rejoin the trail. It didn't take them long to catch up with the wagon. They quickly transferred Beefsteak and made him comfortable.

'Right, get moving and don't stop for anything. Me and Cal are going to ambush Parry and his men from that bluff.'

'I'm comin' with you,' Al said.

'No. We need you and Beefsteak to take care of Josh. The undertaker should be at the livery by now. And you guard the ladies with your lives, you got that? Make sure the Bar-Q is clear before you go in.' Mitch looked at Ellie-Rae and saw a tear roll down her cheek. She wiped it away quickly and smiled at Mitch. 'Be careful and come back,' she said.

'I will, and that's a promise,' Mitch said. 'Now get movin'.'

Mitch and Cal watched as the wagon lumbered forward,

then as one, they wheeled their horses round and headed for the bluff, leaving the trail, cutting diagonally to their target. On reaching the bluff they checked their ammunition and weapons – even though they knew they were well armed. They reached the crest of the bluff with minutes to spare: Parry and his three cohorts were galloping now, intent on catching up with the wagon and killing all those on it – and in particular, Maria. The rest was just a bonus, leaving no witnesses. Parry smiled at the thought: his plan was coming to fruition.

Then two rifle shots shook Parry out of his reverie. He looked behind him, and there were only two men still riding with him and one riderless horse.

'Where the hell did that come from?' Parry yelled.

'Can only be one place, boss. That bluff. The only high ground for miles that I can see.'

Parry dug his spurs in and urged his horse to run even faster. He had as much respect for animals as he did humans, which was none at all.

Another shot rang out and Parry was left with one man and two riderless horses.

'Nice shot Mitch,' Cal said. 'Pity they're out of range now, but that's put the odds well in our favour.'

'Let's mount up and finish this once and for all,' Mitch said, sliding down the sandy bluff to his horse. Cal followed seconds later. Both men then got back on the trail and gave chase.

'We can only be about ten or twelve miles from the ranch. If any of the men there are still alive they'll hear us coming,' Mitch said, but he didn't sound convincing – even to himself.

'We'll catch 'em,' Cal said. 'Sure as eggs is eggs their time is almost up!'

'We got six men including us – I'm not counting Beefsteak, he'll have to stay in the ranch house with Ellie-Rae and Maria. If the worst comes to the worst, they'll all have weapons, but that's looking on the dark side,' Mitch was really thinking out loud.

'Let's get back on the trail,' Cal said. 'We might be able to finish this before we reach the Bar-Q.'

'Yeah,' Mitch agreed. 'We got 'em sandwiched close now, as long as Al and the men don't shoot us,' he grinned.

But it was a worried grin.

Maria was tending to Beefsteak's leg.

'It's not broken,' she said.

'Tole you so!' Beefsteak looked smug.

'But it is badly bruised. You might not be able to walk for a few days,' she added.

'I can still fire a gun, though,' Beefsteak said. 'Prop me up at the back of the wagon and git my rifle,' he said.

It was Al who spoke next. 'We got five men with rifles and enough ammunition to hold off a whole army.'

'Excuse me,' Ellie Rae interrupted, 'you also have Maria and me!'

'Yeah, but you're. . . .'

'Women? Is that what you were gonna say?' Ellie Rae had fire in her eyes as she glared at Al.

'Well, er, no and, maybe, but I was thinking more of you reloading the guns so our fire power isn't reduced while we reload.'

'That makes sense,' Maria said.

'I guess so,' a deflated Ellie Rae agreed.

'OK, the ammo is in that crate, the .45s go into both the Colt handguns and the Winchester rifles, so there's no confusion as to what goes where,' Al said.

'Right,' Beefsteak started, 'get the crate behind me, and you two gals keep low and behind the crate.'

Ellie Rae glared when Beefsteak called them 'gals', but didn't say anything.

'I just caught a glimpse of Mitch and Cal,' Beefsteak said, 'so they're OK as far as I can tell. Different story for Parry: he's only got one rider with him.' Beefsteak chuckled. 'Looks like those two shots were on target,' Beefsteak chuckled some more.

Al had tethered his horse to the side of the wagon and clambered aboard the flat back beside Beefsteak.

'I reckon we can take 'em both out,' Al said: his confidence was growing at the thought of the odds of six to two in their favour, and that it could only reach one outcome.

Parry was thinking fast. He had enemies in front and behind him, so he had to make a plan – and quickly. The desert was slowly giving way to patches of grass, which was a bonus for the horses as the ground was harder and they could gallop faster.

Parry quickly made up his mind, and veered his horse to the left, off the trail and heading diagonally towards the Bar-Q. He knew the wagon couldn't leave the trail, so he would only have the two riders behind him to contend with. If he could make it to the ranch he'd have a better

153

chance in a shoot-out than here in the open. Hal Jones, his right-hand man, was still with him, and Parry had every confidence in his shooting ability. He'd seen it in action many times.

Parry looked back and saw the two riders still on his trail, while ahead he could vaguely see the outline of the ranch house and barns. So close now, Parry could almost taste the ranch.

He'd win this battle.

'They've left the trail,' Beefsteak yelled out.

'Makes no difference,' Al said. 'Mitch and Cal have followed them.'

'The difference is, they'll get to the Bar-Q long before we do,' Beefsteak stated.

'How many men do you think we have there?' Al asked.

'Impossible to say,' Beefsteak replied. 'Neither can we guess how many men Parry has there. We'll just have to hope and pray we got the upper hand. At least Mitch and Cal will be there.'

Gunshots interrupted further conversation. At least a dozen shots were heard and then silence. It was over a minute before anyone spoke.

'Who . . . who do you think was shooting?' Ellie Rae asked, knowing even before anyone answered that they knew as much as she did.

Which was nothing.

Parry and Hal were firing blindly at Mitch and Cal. Riding west towards the Bar-Q, the sun, still low in the sky, almost blinded them as it shone from a perfectly blue sky.

For Mitch and Cal, it was the opposite. They could see Parry and Hal quite clearly, but didn't see the point of wasting ammunition. It would be a very lucky shot for them to hit anybody from a galloping horse.

'They're heading for the Bar-Q,' said Cal.

'Parry still figures he's gonna take it over,' Mitch called out. 'He's in for a big surprise.'

'You reckon any hands would have returned by now?' Cal asked.

'Doubt it, it's a long haul and it looked like ol' Josh had sent the whole herd, take a bunch of men to handle that lot. Must be near on 1,000 head.'

Cal whistled. 'That's a lot of beef.'

Mitch had slowed up to a canter. 'No point in overtiring the horses. We know where he's going, we'll take them out, there.' Mitch grinned at Cal.

Automatically, they both began to check their weapons, even though both men knew that their rifles and pistols were fully loaded.

'Reckon we should head south aways,' Mitch said. 'They'll be expectin' us to be right behind them.'

'Good thinking,' Cal replied and both men started south, getting nearer and nearer to both the Bar-Q and Maria, Ellie-Rae, Al and Beefsteak.

'Doubt we'll see the wagon for a while,' Mitch said. 'I just hope that when they get to the Bar-Q it'll all be over.

'Amen to that,' Cal said.

Parry and Hal had reached the Bar-Q. They dismounted,

shut their horses in the barn and took cover, awaiting the arrival of the two men who had been following them.

The sun was high now, and their vision towards the east had improved considerably, but of the two riders, there was no sign.

'Where the hell are they,' croaked Parry as he scanned the terrain.

'I reckon they're circling us,' Hal replied.

'Splitting up and coming to us from the north and south?' Parry pondered, and rubbed the stubble on his chin.

'Makes sense, to me.' Hal said. 'It's what I'd do.'

'You're right Hal. Let's get to the rear of the ranch house, they won't expect us to be there,' Parry said.

'Might be a good idea if we split up as well. I'll take the back of the barn.'

'Sounds good to me,' Parry said, 'let's go.'

Mitch and Cal dismounted and ground tethered their horses. Taking out their rifles and putting their saddlebags, loaded with ammunition, over their shoulders, they walked towards the Bar-Q.

'No sign of horses,' Mitch said, 'and the stable doors are closed.'

'Well, could mean they rode in the barn, or it could mean they just put the horses in there and are hiding out someplace, ready to bushwhack us,' Cal said.

'I think the bushwhack idea is the way to go. Parry's a bully, and bullies don't like face-to-face unless they got plenty of back-up,' Mitch said.

Cal laughed. 'Ain't that the truth!'

156

'OK,' Mitch said, 'I suggest we split up. You take the barn from the rear, I'll take the back of the house. There's no way they can get into the house, so they gotta be hiding where they can see us.'

Cal held his hand out. 'Take care out there,' he said and the two men shook hands.

'You too, Cal. See you after the show.'

The two men went their separate ways, each man wondering whether they'd meet again. Mitch ran at a crouch towards the ranch house; on reaching it, he got his breath back and kept his back hard up against the wall. He edged his way left till he got to the side of the house, and took a careful peek around the corner.

Nothing there. Slowly, he edged his way to the rear of the ranch house, his trigger finger itching.

At the same time, Cal made it to the barn and held his breath listening for any sound of movement. It was deathly quiet.

He moved to the rear of the barn, and as he leant forward to see if the coast was clear, a shot rang out, nicking his right shoulder. It stung like hell, but was only a flesh wound, and he still had time to get off two shots blindly.

He heard a yelp, and knew he'd found a target. Then it was silent again.

Cal got down on all fours, then on to his belly. He crawled forwards and slowly stuck his hat out. No shot came. Either the guy was savvy to this trick, or he was playing possum.

On the other hand, thought Cal, he could be dead. He left his hat on the ground and stood, and slowly, again peered round the back of the barn.

He saw the body sprawled in the dirt. Even from this distance he could see the blood forming a puddle around the man's head. He carefully walked towards the body to make sure the man was dead, then turned his attention to the ranch house.

He hadn't seen which way Mitch had gone and he sure didn't want to walk into one of Mitch's bullets. While he was deliberating, he heard the wagon thundering down the trail towards the Bar-Q. Risking his own life, Cal stood at the trail end and waved his arms above his head in an attempt to at least slow it down. Beefsteak got the message and told Al to rein in. Slowly, the wagon ground to a halt.

Ellie-Rae and Maria were the first to leap to the ground. Maria walked straight towards Cal and said, 'You are hurt, señor,' she said. Doc Mayweather came over with his bag. 'Soon sort that out,' he said gruffly, but he was smiling as he said it.

'Where's Mitch?' Ellie asked.

'He's behind the ranch house – with Parry.'

Ellie went to run to the ranch house, but Cal stopped her. 'I don't know what's going on back there, but there's been no shots fired and. . . .'

Almost simultaneously two shots echoed around the ranch compound.

A shadow appeared from behind the ranch house. It lengthened, then disappeared instantly.

'What the. . . .' Cal said softly.

Cautiously he made his way to the ranch house, keeping close to the side of the house. He reached the

Mayweather had patched up his shoulder – again – he,

Ellie-Rae wouldn't let go of Mitch, and after Doc

He smiled at her and she smiled back.

and, Cal thought, she sure was a handsome woman.

much older than Cal, he knew that, but you couldn't tell,

the first time, Cal looked at Maria the woman. She was

'Sure thing, ma . . . Maria.' Cal went bright red. For

ma'am. My name is Maria.'

'Only one condition,' Maria said. 'You never call me

'It'd be an honour and a pleasure, ma'am.'

'I don't suppose,' she started. . . .

stared at Cal, her intention quite obvious.

'Not quite,' Maria said. 'I don't have a foreman.' She

'Yup. The Bar-Q is safe now, Miss Maria.' Cal said.

'Sure is. I guess Hal is, too.'

'Parry dead, Mitch?' Cal asked.

'That was worth getting shot for,' Mitch grinned.

leaned forwards and kissed him on the lips.

'Almost!' Ellie showed mock annoyance. Then she

smiling.

'That was almost worth getting shot for,' said Mitch,

on his cheek.

Ellie-Rae ran to Mitch's side and kissed him tenderly

again!'

bring your bag Doc, he's been hit in the shoulder –

'It's OK,' Cal called back to the others, 'it's Mitch,

'The same bloody shoulder,' Mitch said and grinned.

shoulder.

eagled in the dirt, blood seeping slowly from his left

another shot. But to his relief he saw it was Mitch, spread-

back and peered round the corner, expecting to hear

THE BATTLE FOR THE BAR-Q

Beefsteak, Al and Aloishus Wainwright sat in the back of the wagon. Aloishus then opened a bottle of the finest Scotch whisky.

Tomorrow they would bury Josh Winters in the Calvary graveyard with all due respect.